# HOPE

## A GOING HOME NOVEL

### A. AMERICAN
### G. MICHAEL HOPF

Copyright © 2016 G. Michael Hopf & A. American
No part of this book may be reproduced in any manner whatsoever without permission except in the case of brief quotations embodied in critical articles or reviews.
For information contact:
geoff@gmichaelhopf.com
www.gmichaelhopf.com
All rights reserved.
ISBN: 10: 1530257662
ISBN-13: 978- 1530257669

# DEDICATION

TO THE MILLIONS OF MISSING CHILDREN
WE SHALL NEVER REST UNTIL YOU ARE FOUND

"In the end, it's not the years in your life that count.

It's the life in your years."

- Abraham Lincoln

## CHAPTER ONE

"Hope is the word which God has written on the brow of every man." – Victor Hugo

### Descanso, CA

Charlotte wasn't sure if it was the throaty rumble of the truck engine pulling into their driveway or her father's voice ordering her and her little sister to go hide that she heard first. Not questioning him, she took Hope firmly by the hand and raced upstairs.

"What's happening, Charlotte?" her sister asked, her voice trembling.

"Somebody's coming and Daddy wants us to hide, like before," Charlotte replied, walking hand in hand into the master bedroom's walk-in closet. "Now just wait here; I'll be right back."

"No," Hope pleaded. "I'm just going to get my diary, I need it."

Hope gripped Charlotte's hand tighter. Her eyes widened as she again begged for Charlotte to stay. "I'm scared. Don't go."

"Hope, I'm just running into my room. I'll be right back."

"No," Hope replied as her little fingers squeezed hard.

"Hope, you're six; you're a big girl now. I'll just

be a sec," Charlotte said and pulled away. She closed the closet door and ran to her bedroom just down the hall.

Charlotte could hear voices outside her window. Curious, she peered out to see an old pickup truck, and circling it were five men. Her father, not a small man, towered over them all. He was engaged in a heated conversation with a man she recognized seeing once before.

"I told you I don't know where it is," Charlotte's father hollered.

"Yeah, you do. You're the only one who would," the man replied.

"I told you already, I don't know, plus why would I ever cross you?"

"It's very easy, just tell me where it is and I'll let you and your little family live."

Charlotte watched the man spit out a large wad of tobacco juice. He grinned and said, "I'll give you one more chance, and if you don't tell us, I'll go in there, rip out your two pretty little girls, and have my boys here do unimaginable things to them."

"I told you I didn't take it."

Charlotte's heart pumped heavily and her hand trembled with fear.

A commotion broke out as Charlotte's father produced a gun and waved it in front of the man. "Go away now, or I'll shoot you!"

Calmly the man stepped to the side and pulled out his own pistol and immediately shot Charlotte's father in the chest.

Charlotte gasped and stumbled backwards at the sight of her father falling to the ground. She tripped over the edge of the bed and hit the floor hard.

The creak of the front door hit her ears.

The man hollered, "Tear the place apart, boys. I want what is mine!"

Charlotte scrambled to her feet and sprinted from her bedroom towards the master bedroom, with her pink diary in her hand.

Back in the closet, she found Hope whimpering behind a row of clothes.

She closed the door and tucked up next to her.

A small box lay next to her; inside was a flashlight. She took it out and turned it on.

The bright light lit the dark space.

With a crackling voice, Hope asked, "What was that sound?"

Charlotte didn't reply; she opened her diary and began to write.

*January 21*

*Dear Mommy,*

*The bad men came back. Daddy said they wouldn't and they did. Me and Hope are hiding in your closet.*

"Charlotte, where's Daddy?"

"Ssh, not so loud," Charlotte ordered.

"I want Dada." Hope began to sob. "I'm scared."

Charlotte looked up to see tears streaming down Hope's plump rosy cheeks. Knowing she had to comfort her but still determined to jot down what she could, she set the flashlight down in her lap and put her arm around Hope.

Hope melted into Charlotte's chest and cried.

*Mommy, I miss you. Where are you? How come you never came home? Daddy says it's because you were far away when the power went out. Are you mad at me? Did I do something to make you mad?*

Voices boomed from what sounded like the hallway.

Hope quivered.

Charlotte looked up at the door. She feared that at any moment it would open and they'd die like her father.

Looking back down at the eggshell-white paper, she began to write again.

*If I made you mad, I'm sorry. Please come home, we need you.*

The voices grew louder.

Hope's tears continued to flow and her body shook with fear.

Charlotte paused her writing. She asked if there was more to write. Had she written enough? Her father had told her to begin the diary soon after everything stopped working so she could have a connection with her mother and as a way for her to express the emotions she was feeling. She had taken to it almost instantly and found solace in the words she wrote daily. Charlotte looked at it as a form of communication, a series of letters and notes to her mother, who had never returned from a trip back to the Midwest she had taken a day before the world came to a grinding halt.

"Where's Dada? I want Dada," Hope moaned.

Not wanting to tell Hope what she saw, she lied, "I don't know where Dada is." This lie to her sister prompted her to reveal the truth to her mother.

*Daddy died today. The bad men killed him. They shot him out in front of the house for no reason. Hope is crying. She's scared.*

*Oh no, the bad men are now in your room. I'm scared. I think we're going to die. I don't want to die, Mommy, I don't want to die.*

The sound of heavy footfalls stopped just outside the closet door.

Charlotte questioned whether she had locked the door. To be sure, she reached up to verify and found the door unlocked. Her gut clenched and sweat formed on her brow. Delicately she pushed the pin that locked the handle and just in time.

The knob jiggled.

Charlotte slid back further into the closet until

her back was against the wall.

Hope clung to her waist and whimpered.

Softly, Charlotte said, "Ssh."

The knob jiggled harder and the pressure of someone outside the door weighed against it.

Remembering the small revolver her father had left in the box just for this type of emergency, Charlotte reached in and grabbed it. The steel felt cold against the hot skin of her palm and the weight was heavy. She wrapped both her small hands around the grip and pointed it at the door.

"Hey, the door is locked!" a man barked from the other side of the door.

Hope and Charlotte drew closer, if that was even possible.

Charlotte's hand shook, making the loose cylinder of the revolver rattle.

"Kick it open!" another man's voice boomed. This was the voice of the man who'd shot Charlotte's father.

Charlotte tensed her body, waiting for the door to come crashing in at any moment, but nothing happened.

Voices called from further in the house.

The shadow underneath the door disappeared, gone as fast as it had appeared.

Charlotte gulped hard. A steady sweat poured down her face.

# HOPE

Hollers now echoed from the opposite side of the house.

"Are the bad men gone?" Hope whispered.

"I don't know," Charlotte said, lowering the revolver, her arms aching.

"I'm scared."

"Me too."

"Where's Dada?" Hope asked, lifting her head from Charlotte's lap.

"I don't know," Charlotte said, again not able to tell Hope the truth.

"Is Dada dead?"

Charlotte opened her mouth to reply but froze.

"Charlotte, is Dada dead?"

"I don't know."

"I heard something, was it a gun?"

Heavy footfalls came again and stopped just outside the door. "Open it up the old-fashioned way!"

"Will do!" a man replied.

Charlotte shook, her arms outstretched with the revolver.

The door exploded open.

Both girls screamed in terror.

The man froze when he saw the muzzle of the revolver pointed at him. "Now, take it easy there, little one," he said, his hand held out and motioning for her to put it down.

Charlotte's eyes were as wide as saucers. She placed her index finger on the trigger and began to apply pressure.

"Put the gun down, okay, sweetheart. Don't do nothin' stupid."

A second man appeared and chuckled when he saw the two girls. He turned to the first man and said with a pat on his back, "The boss will be happy."

The first man held him back and warned, "Dude, she has a gun."

"I know, I ain't blind, but I don't think that pretty little thing will do anything to me," he said with a toothy grin.

Charlotte's arms began to shake vigorously from a combination of fear and fatigue.

"I don't know, man, she has a look in her eye," the first man said, taking a step back and out of the aim of Charlotte.

"She's just a little girl," the second man said and took another step inside the closet.

"Leave us alone!" Charlotte screamed.

"What's your name?" the second man asked as he knelt down a few feet from her.

"Leave!"

"We won't hurt you, I promise."

Tears flowed down Charlotte's face. "Leave."

Hope was crying uncontrollably.

With his hand out in front of him, the man

repeated, "We won't hurt you, I promise."

"You killed…"

"Your father didn't cooperate; he was a stupid man. Don't be like your daddy, girl."

"Dada!" Hope wailed.

"Leave or I'll shoot!" Charlotte barked.

"It would be irresponsible for us to leave you here alone. There's a lot of bad people out there."

"Leave!"

The man shifted quickly to the right, but with his left hand he snatched the revolver and twisted it out of Charlotte's hand.

Charlotte and Hope both curled up tight and recoiled as far as they could, their backs planted firmly against the cold wall.

The man stood, looked at the other man, and said, "If we don't find the other shit, at least the day wasn't a total loss."

## CHAPTER TWO

"Hope is the pillar that holds up the world. Hope is the dream of a waking man." – Pliny the Elder

El Centro, CA

Neal opened his eyes and stared towards the popcorn-white ceiling. His insomnia was becoming unbearable, but what were his choices? He thought about taking the sleeping pills he had found, but the thought of drugging himself just felt wrong.

The full moon cast its light through his bedroom window and provided him a reprieve from the intense darkness that he was accustomed to living with during these late hours. Taking advantage of a bad situation, he pressed his eyes closed and ran through the plan for the day in his mind. He was someone who believed in creative visualization and had done it often during his college football days. Now instead of visualizing successful catches, he'd process each step he would make, each turn and every doorway he'd shadow, with the outcome being positive with his safe return.

Finished with his exercise, he glanced towards the darkened digital alarm clock. It was a habit he hadn't been able to kick even though the red glowing lights hadn't shown for eight months. His guess was it was sometime after three in the morning, his normal wake-up time these days.

Putting his attention back on the ceiling, he began to recite the things he was grateful for. Like his visual exercise, this had become another ritual and one that kept him a bit sane and thinking positive. His wife, Karen, was always the first on the list he'd think of, not because she was lying next to him sleeping but because he wouldn't have been able to keep it together much less survive the past months without her. Second was his eight-year-old daughter, Beth. She was the twinkle in his eye, the light of his life, and many people often referred to her as his twin. There was no mistaking her as his daughter. Karen would often joke that the only reason she knew Beth was hers was because she gave birth to her. Third on his list was Carlos, his neighbor and friend for many years. Together, they had managed to secure food, water and additional supplies. Carlos was a mechanic by trade and fortunately for them also collected old classic hot rods, which came in handy since many modern vehicles had ceased to work.

While he went through his list, many faces of those he had known would come to mind, other neighbors, co-workers and even the familiar faces he'd see on a regular basis at the store or coffee shop. All gone or not seen since the blackout. All of his and Carlos' neighbors had packed up and left, many on foot. Their final destination was the rumored FEMA camp in Yuma, Arizona. If there was anything that remained a sure thing, it was the rumor mill. Within hours of the blackout, rumors flew. Many gathered that a terrorist attack had occurred, and practically thinking, it made sense. Soon the rumors came that the federal government was mobilizing a response to the crisis and establishing relief camps in Riverside. This rumor was proven fact when a small convoy from the Department of Homeland Security passed through, plastering leaflets. Not long afterwards came the US Postal Service. They moved through town, taking a survey of the residents and giving them instructions. Like a levee breaking, the residents of El Centro, a small desert city one hundred and eighteen miles east of San Diego, flooded out, all headed for Yuma and the promise of salvation.

Neal and Carlos resisted the call to leave. Neal and Carlos avoided the mailmen and their DHS security teams. With everyone gone, they factored their ability to sustain themselves was greater with a majority of the population gone. Their theory proved correct. With most people gone, they found an abundance of food, water and supplies. As the days turned to weeks then into months, they had become so accustomed to their new lives that the world of before seemed like a dream. The abandoned cars that littered the highway and streets became a nuisance not a reminder. When the water stopped flowing, the acres upon acres of crops that surrounded the city had surrendered the green crops to the desert. The massive transmission towers were silent; the crackling of electricity that used to flow through them shut off that day and never came back on. They now stood as relics of an age that neither man believed was coming back. Everything around them represented a time of ease, abundance and in many ways decadence.

Neal began his daily ritual of gratitude because he wanted to remain positive but also because he knew the day of coasting would come to an end. They had managed to survive without the problems many had suffered. Not a week would go by without them encountering a wandering pack of people. For the most part they kept their distance, but occasionally they had conversations. The news from around the country wasn't good. The blackout had affected the entire nation from coast to coast. Everything was down; the entire electrical grid had collapsed along with most devices that had solid-state components. With the grid, society itself fell. The federal government's response hadn't been what the people expected, with rumors of people being gathered and systematically removed or, as some wanderers put it, people had just disappeared.

Carlos and Neal listened to the stories and didn't know what to believe. All they knew was their decision to stay had worked, but the day would come when something really bad would happen. This thought would nag Neal daily. Like a hovering mosquito that wouldn't go away regardless of how many times you batted the air, the dark images of his family suffering would plague his mind. He had no issues with something happening to him, he even could tolerate Karen getting hurt, but any image of Beth in trouble made him nauseous. It was a parent's responsibility to protect their children and die before them. If there was one thing that haunted him, it was that, losing Beth.

"I can hear you thinking," Karen mumbled under her breath.

"You're awake?"

Karen rolled onto her back and snuggled up to Neal. "Yeah, been awake for a while."

"You good?" Neal asked.

"It's never going to be the same, is it?"

"Nope."

"It's just so weird. You know, I don't miss the old world."

Neal turned his head and asked, "Really? I don't believe that for one second. You loved your reality shows, and I swear you went through withdrawals without your Starbucks macchiatos."

"Reality TV, no, but yes, I do miss my Starbucks."

"I miss ice cream. I can see it now; hell, I can taste it when I think about chocolate peanut butter Haagen-Dazs."

"And that, I miss that too," Karen mused and drew closer.

"Does it sound odd to say I miss McDonald's French fries?" Neal joked.

"McDonald's? When did you eat McDonald's?"

"Well..."

"Secrets? Now I hear about dark secrets?"

"I wouldn't call grabbing a large fry now and then a dark secret."

"What else have you kept from me?" Karen prodded.

"Besides all my mistresses, nothing," he joked.

She jabbed him in the side with her elbow. "You better be kidding."

"Ouch, I am, geez."

"Anything else?"

"No, no other secrets."

"Not that, anything you really miss."

"A good sci-fi movie."

"I miss pizza. Don't ask me why, but a nice thin crust with roasted garlic, sausage, onion and mushroom sounds good right about now."

"Pizza at three a.m.?"

"Anytime, God, my mouth is watering thinking about it."

Neal leaned close and gave her a full kiss on the mouth.

She returned his kiss and began to caress his body. She stopped, pulled away slightly, and said, "I don't miss the spare tire you were carrying. You look and feel good," she purred.

"If only I knew the apocalypse diet was the one way to bring back my lean and mean twenty something look, I would've done it long ago."

She ran her hand across his chest and belly. "Wow."

He leaned in and kissed her again, this time more firmly and passionately.

"I'm scared," whispered Beth from the doorway.

Neal and Karen jumped.

"What is it, sweetheart?" Karen asked.

Beth pushed the cracked door fully open and entered the moonlit room. "I had a bad dream."

Karen got out of bed, approached Beth, and gave her a warm embrace. "Come on, honey, let's get you back in bed."

Beth stood firm and asked, "Can I sleep with you and Daddy?"

Karen looked towards Neal, who sat up and shrugged his shoulders.

"No, honey, you should sleep in your own bed," Karen replied. Normally Karen would have said yes, but tonight she hoped to return and continue the intimate moment she and Neal had been having.

"No, Mommy, I'm really scared," Beth resisted.

"Come, Beth, let's go back to bed. It was just a bad dream."

"I dreamed you died," Beth cried out with tears following.

Karen knelt and gave her another embrace. "It's okay, sweetie. It was just a bad dream, nothing more."

"I saw you, you were there, dead," Beth said, pointing towards the bed.

Karen petted her hair and attempted to comfort her.

"Your eyes were open, but they just stared. You were dead, Mommy, you were dead," Beth cried.

"Karen, it's okay. She can jump in bed with us," Neal said softly.

"Come on, baby, jump in bed with us," Karen said, taking her by the hand and escorting her to the bed.

Beth and Karen both got in the bed with Beth snuggled between them.

Neal leaned over and gave Beth a dozen small kisses on her cheeks and forehead. "So, Mommy and I were talking about what we've missed since the power stopped. So far on the list we have ice cream, sci-fi movies, French fries, pizza…"

Excited to take part in the conversation, Beth blurted out, "Mac and cheese."

"Yeah, mac and cheese, I miss that too," Neal said.

"But not with any of that yucky stuff you put on it," Beth countered.

"What yucky stuff?" Neal asked.

"The hot sauce," Beth replied.

"You just need to acquire the taste, that's all," Neal said, defending his use of Tapatio hot sauce.

Karen tickled Beth and said, "I agree with you, yucky."

"Whatever, all I know is hot sauce is proof that God loves us."

Karen rolled her eyes even though Neal couldn't see. It wasn't a gesture out of contempt but one of love. She and Neal had met nine years before and one thing that she loved about his personality was his humor. He was the one man that made her truly laugh.

"I miss my friends," Beth said.

"You do?" Neal asked.

"Yeah, I miss Ella the most."

"I know, you two were besties," Karen said, rubbing Beth's arm.

"Are they still alive?" Beth asked.

The question threw Karen and Neal. "Why would you ask that?" Neal asked.

"I heard you and Mom talking about seeing people dead and…"

Karen leaned in and asked, "And what?"

"I heard Daddy say something about wondering if the Reynolds and your other friends were dead."

Karen sighed. "We were just talking."

Neal sat up, cleared his throat, and replied bluntly, "Honey, the world has changed and not exactly for the best. It's different and, well…"

"What were you about to say?" Karen asked him.

"It's time we were honest with her."

"No, she's just a little girl."

"Karen, she needs to know, not the gruesome details, but we can't shield her from the realities out there."

"No," Karen insisted.

"Karen, I'm just going to chat with her. She's going to find out one way or another and I'd rather have her hear it from me directly than to overhear me and not understand the context."

Karen thought for a second before replying, "How about we discuss what you're thinking of saying?"

Neal also paused before responding. "Fine."

"Tell me," Beth urged.

"No, your mother's right. We both will discuss

what's happening out there, but do it later."

"C'mon."

"No, now get some sleep," Karen said.

Beth crossed her arms and grunted.

Neal leaned in and kissed her on the forehead. "Get some sleep."

Beth grumbled.

He got closer and whispered into her ear, "And I don't think Ella and her parents are dead. I was just wondering. After a lot of thought I came to the conclusion they were fine. Ella's daddy is a smart guy; I'm sure he got to Ella's grandparents' house safe and sound."

"You sure?"

"Yes, now close your eyes. I need you bright eyed and bushy tailed in the morning, you've gotta help Mommy inventory the pantry."

"Okay, love you, Dada."

"Love you too."

"Love you, Mama."

Karen kissed her and whispered, "Love you, baby."

Neal rolled onto his back and immediately thoughts of the Reynolds came rushing in. He didn't know for sure if they were safe, but telling Beth they were did ease her mind. Was that right for him to do? Being a parent was not an easy job, and those who thought it was were usually not parents. When you first discovered you'd be a parent, you really didn't know what to expect. Yes, many people experienced joy but also fear came. Would you be a good parent? Would you have all the answers? Would your kids grow up to be good people? There had been many books written on parenting, but were any of them correct? How did you talk to a child about the apocalypse? he asked himself. Just how did you begin that conversation, over a family dinner? 'Hi, Beth, the world as you know it just ended and you may not survive. Do you want rice or beans?' He had thought before of discussing what happened with her, but he never could find that right moment. Now with her asking questions like she just did, he knew it was the time.

It didn't take long for Beth to fall back to sleep. Her heavy and rhythmic breathing gave him peace, but it was now time for him to get up and prepare for the long day ahead.

## CHAPTER THREE

"Hope in reality is the worst of all evils because it prolongs the torments of man." – Friedrich Nietzsche

### Guatay, CA

Charlotte woke abruptly when the door opened. She opened her eyes, but the canvas sack that covered her head prevented her from seeing. She squirmed on the floor as best she could with her arms bound behind her and her legs tied tightly together.

Voices hit her ears. She couldn't make out if they were the same men who took her and Hope.

"Hope, you there?" she asked.

No reply.

"Hope?"

"She's not here; she's in another room."

"Please don't hurt us, please," she pleaded.

A hand touched her arm.

She scooted away.

"I won't hurt you, I promise. I'm here to bring you food," the man said.

This voice was different than the others.

The man again reached and touched her arm, this time more gently. "I won't hurt you, I swear."

There was something in his voice that soothed

her. She quit moving and allowed him to sit her upright.

The man removed the bag from her head.

Charlotte squinted and looked away when the light of the early morning hit her eyes. When her vision adjusted, she looked around to get acquainted with her new surroundings and with the man.

He was kneeling down just feet in front of her.

"Where's my sister?"

"She's just in the other room. She's fine, well, not exactly fine, who could be in this situation?" the man said.

"I want to see her," Charlotte insisted.

"Are you hungry?" the man asked.

Charlotte shook her head.

"I've got some food here. I'll leave it, and you can eat when you're hungry, okay?" the man said, setting a plate next to her.

Charlotte kicked the plate.

"That wasn't nice," the man said. "But I understand." He picked up an orange that had rolled off and placed it back on the plate. "Here's some water too. You need to stay hydrated."

"I want my sister," Charlotte barked.

Another man stepped in the small cinder-block room and asked, "You need help, Drew?"

Charlotte recognized this man as the one who had disarmed her.

"I got this," Drew replied, his gaze still on Charlotte.

"Let me know, that one is feisty," the man at the door said.

"She's fine, just scared," Drew countered.

"Whatever, hurry up, we have to make a run for the boss," the man said and walked away.

"I need you to eat and drink. You need to stay strong for your sister."

Charlotte glared.

Drew reached towards her.

Charlotte kicked his hands.

"If you're going to eat, I need to untie your arms, and I'll untie your legs so you can at least pace around the room."

Charlotte thought for a moment and realized she didn't have any power, and if he was going to hurt her, he could do so regardless. She turned slightly and offered him her hands.

Drew untied her hands and then her feet. "All better."

Charlotte still couldn't find her ability to speak unless it was about Hope.

Seeing nothing but fear coming from Charlotte, Drew tried to calm her with casual conversation. "Your sister told me your name is Charlotte. That's a beautiful name. Mine is Drew, short for Andrew, but no one's called me that since I was a kid."

Charlotte nodded.

Time wasn't his ally, so he decided to alleviate her fear with some reassuring words. "I'm one of the good guys. I won't hurt you, and I'll make sure they don't either."

"I want to see Hope," Charlotte blurted out.

"I'll see about making that happen."

"What are you going to do with us?"

Drew looked down; his long black hair fell around his face. "Nothing if I can help it."

"What do they want to do with us?"

He looked up and said, "You have to trust me; I'll keep you safe." Drew got up quickly and exited the room.

## CHAPTER FOUR

"Neither should a ship rely on one small anchor, nor should life rest on a single hope." – Epictetus

### El Centro, CA

Carlos slid the blade of his Spyderco Police model folding knife across the whetstone. The gritty sound the steel made crossing the stone brought back fond memories of his childhood. Like a skipping record, the voice of his father would repeat the process of sharpening a blade. After a dozen passes, he gently touched the edge with his thumb. "Just about right."

He ran the blade a half dozen more times across the stone then closed it and placed it back in his right-hand pocket of his blue jeans.

He glanced at his old Timex watch before removing it and winding it for the day. It too brought back memories, as it was a gift from his father. The watch had been inexpensive and wasn't worth much, but to Carlos it was priceless, as it represented his father's struggle for freedom many years ago in Cuba. That watch had been with him during his fight against Fidel Castro and journeyed with him across the ocean as they fled the island nation to find a new home in America.

Carlos knew nothing of his father's struggles

except for the few stories detailed over the years. The watch came to Carlos on his sixteenth birthday, but it wasn't until later in life did he appreciate its significance. He thought that only when someone experienced true misery or suffering did they gain a real understanding of how precious life and happiness were.

Carlos missed his father and wished he were with him and his family. Having a man like him during this current strife would be beneficial, but alas, it couldn't be. His father had passed ten years back, but he didn't leave alone. He had arrived in a new land with nothing and no one, but the day he closed his eyes for the last time, he was surrounded by the loving family he had created.

With his knife sharpened and his watch set, Carlos was ready to tackle the day ahead. He exited the garage, which doubled as his shop, and entered the house. The first thing that hit his nostrils was the savory smell of fried eggs. Instantly his stomach grumbled and mouth watered. He weaved through the hallway until he reached the small kitchen; there he found his wife, Natalie, and his son, Ricardo.

"Good morning," Natalie said, not taking her attention away from the eggs cooking.

"How's the fuel looking on the stove?" Carlos asked, referring to the gas canister on the old Coleman camping stove.

"This tank is half full, but I have two more. Thank God you found that stash," Natalie replied.

"Dad, when can I come with you?" Ricardo asked, his somber face buried in his hands.

Carlos walked over to him and rubbed his shoulders. "Soon, very soon."

"That's what you always say," Ricardo grumbled.

Carlos sat down next to him and leaned close. "Ricky, my son, it's dangerous out there. I need to make sure you're capable of handling yourself first, plus your mother—"

Cutting Carlos off, Natalie interjected, "Will never allow it, period."

"I'm eleven, I can shoot a gun, and you've taught me how to fight with a knife," Ricardo moaned.

Carlos felt for his son. He knew too well the desire to see what was happening outside the comfort and relative safety of their small community. He patted Ricardo on the head and said, "Soon, I promise."

Ricardo pulled away and, in frustration, got up from the table and stormed off.

"Ricky, sit back down," Carlos urged.

Ricardo didn't listen and disappeared down the hall.

"I'm going to have to get him schooled up and soon, you know that," Carlos stated flatly.

"He's just a boy."

"Those are old sensibilities; times are different. He needs to see and experience the world when we can have some control."

"No."

"Natalie, you think you're protecting him, but he has to see it before it comes here unannounced."

Natalie carefully placed perfectly cooked eggs over easy on a plate and turned to face Carlos. "He's not ready."

"I agree, but soon he will be."

She stepped over to Carlos and set the plate down. "I'm not ready for that."

Carlos took her hand and said, "Trust me; I wouldn't put him in a situation that could get him hurt."

"You don't know that. You even remarked the other day how you know something bad will happen. You sat right there and said we've been lucky but that luck would soon run out. I don't want that luck to run out when you're out there with Ricky."

Carlos sighed. He picked up the fork next to his plate and poked the eggs until the golden thick yolk oozed onto his plate. He lowered his head and breathed in deeply. "They smell delicious."

"And they are, I made them," Natalie joked.

"Where's your dad?" Carlos asked, referring to Natalie's father, who was living with them now.

"Still in bed. He said he wasn't feeling well."

"Hmm, sorry to hear that. I'll call off our run today," Carlos said.

"No, you go. We need you both out there. Pop will get up; he's just feeling tired is all."

"You sure?" Carlos asked, concerned about leaving them with her father not well. While they were gone on runs, Frank kept watch over the families.

"We'll be fine. Now eat while they're hot," Natalie said, turning towards the stove.

As he ate, he couldn't stop thinking about all the bad things that could go wrong, and the thought of Ricardo being in the middle of trouble haunted him, but at the same time he needed him to be prepared and capable. One of the only ways to do that was to get him out on the road. That wasn't going to happen now, but soon, so in the meantime he'd need to keep training him.

Neal press checked the Sig Sauer P239 to ensure he had a round in the chamber before placing the pistol in the holster of his tactical vest. On his hip he carried a Glock 22. It was his main carry pistol, and he loved the .40 caliber; hence why he carried the Sig. That model came in a 9mm, but on one of his outings he came upon the .40-caliber version and made it his backup. He couldn't be described as a gun lover before, but now he wouldn't be caught without one outside the house. The Glock had been his since before, but it mostly remained in a safe in the closet.

The only disadvantage he thought they'd encounter later on was ammunition, but that hadn't come true as of yet. In fact, they hadn't yet had to use their weapons. He and Carlos had a few altercations, but none ever came to gunplay, and for that, he was grateful.

On his vest he carried one sheath knife, a 5.11 CFK, and three magazine pouches, one for each pistol and one for the M4, a Daniel Defense V3 he would take with him on any excursion. Of course, he owed his entire kit, minus the Sig, to Carlos.

Using the basking light of the morning sun, he finished checking his gear and readying himself for another day trip. Today, he and Carlos would push the furthest they had ever gone and go to the southern tip of Brawly, a town north of them. They didn't know what they'd find, but the one resource that would be an issue for them soon was water.

Life in the desert was made bearable by electricity. All the major cities that many were familiar with—Las Vegas, Phoenix and others—were now drying up.

Neal and Carlos both knew their days were numbered in El Centro, but the question remained where to go next?

Feeling confident and ready, Neal entered his house to kiss Karen and Beth goodbye. Like many other rituals, this was one of the most important ones.

Embracing Karen, he squeezed her and whispered, "I love you."

"I love you too," Karen replied softly.

Neal knelt and faced Beth. He gazed into her eyes and with a gentle hand tucked a stray lock of hair behind her ears. "You and Mommy be good."

"Okay."

Neal pulled her close and, like he did with Karen, said, "I love you, never forget that."

"I love you too."

He stood and looked at the only thing that mattered to him. He took a mental picture of the two standing there and stored it in his memory. "I'll be back just before dark."

"Okay," Karen said and nodded slightly.

"You know—"

"I know what to do," Karen said, interrupting him. "Now go, the sooner you leave, the sooner you'll return to us."

"Love you guys," he said and exited the house. Outside, he found Carlos leaning against the car, his arms crossed.

"Were you waiting long?" Neal asked.

"Nope, how's the fam?"

"Good, and yours?"

"Same. Hop in, we've got a long ride ahead of us," Carlos said and slid into the driver's seat of what he affectionately referred to as his 'baby', a black 1966 Lincoln Continental.

Neal got in and took a deep breath. "How is it that this thing always smells so good? Do you have a lifetime supply of air freshener?"

"Something like that," Carlos replied, turning the key. The engine roared to life.

Carlos pulled away from the cul-de-sac. He weaved around the abandoned cars he and Neal had placed in the street to slow down the traffic going into their cul-de-sac. He pulled up just shy of the stop sign at the end so Neal could get out.

Neal exited the car and pulled away a homemade spike strip. Carlos pulled forward. Neal laid the strip back down and ran to the car.

"You ready for a good day?" Carlos asked as Neal sat down.

"I get so nervous leaving them here," Neal lamented.

"Me too, but Natalie's old man is a good shot. He was a jarhead back in the day."

"I know your father-in- law is a solid guy, but I still hate it."

Carlos patted Neal on the leg and said, "They'll be fine." He put the car back in gear and exited the neighborhood by taking a hard right.

"You know, I think this might be pointless," Neal said, his gaze scanning the road ahead.

"We need water, it's that simple," Carlos said.

"But what about fuel, you said that soon the gas will start to go bad."

"It will."

"Then shouldn't we pack up and go."

"Go where?" Carlos asked.

"South, maybe Central America," Neal replied.

"You've heard the rumors like I have. If we happen to make it to the Mexican checkpoints, we'll only be turned around, and that's a big if when saying we'll make it. The road bandits or a roving cartel will probably get us before then. Going south is too risky."

"But those are just rumors," Neal said.

"Then why don't we just go see if the feds will help us at one of those camps," Carlos declared.

"Screw them."

"So you'd rather take your chances with a cartel than your own government?"

Frustrated, Neal remained quiet, his eyes going back and forth on the road.

Carlos weaved the large Lincoln around the abandoned cars that riddled the roadway. "You good?" Carlos asked.

"You know, we could make a run for my sailboat

in San Diego. It's big enough for all of us. We could set sail for South America or Hawaii."

"C'mon, Neal, you even said you weren't the best sailor and that boat was a bit too big for you to handle."

"Taking that boat seems less risky than our other options."

"That's if it's even there anymore."

Neal sighed.

"So Ricky got upset with me again this morning. He wants to come with us so badly, but you know Natalie."

"You can't win."

"Nope."

"I'm getting really nervous. We've got to make a plan, commit to it, and then act," Neal stressed.

"I agree."

Neal brought his right hand to his mouth and was about to nervously chew his nails but stopped short of doing it. It had been years since he quit that habit, but the circumstances rekindled the urge. He put his hand down and gripped his rifle.

"First thing we need to do before we plan any move is get more water."

"It's the stuff of life, they say," Neal joked.

"That it is."

Neal caught sight of a road sign that read BRAWLEY 9 MILES. "Let's just pray we find what we need and get home safe."

"Hey, my friend, have I ever let you down?" Carlos asked.

"No, but we've gone for too long with nothing happening. Our luck has to run out," Neal worried.

"Luck? I don't believe in luck."

"Well, whatever you want to call it, we need more of it."

Carlos patted Neal's shoulder, winked and said, "We'll be fine, brother, we'll be fine."

Two Miles South of Brawley, CA

"Carlos, slow down, slow down!" Neal barked.

Carlos did exactly as he asked and more as he brought the car to a gentle roll before stopping in the middle of the road.

"There, up there, you see it?" Neal asked, pointing to a glimmer in the middle of the road just on the horizon.

Carlos leaned over the steering wheel and squinted. "Where?"

"The glimmering straight ahead."

"I don't see anything."

"Are you serious?"

Carlos leaned further as if the extra inch would bring what he couldn't see into focus.

Neal looked at him and asked, "Are you fucking

blind?"

"I, um, well, my long-distance vision isn't the best," Carlos admitted.

"Christ, man, there's a roadblock up ahead, I bet my life on it."

Carlos reached in the backseat and picked up a small set of binoculars. "When in doubt, zoom in," he joked, placing the optics to his eyes. "Damn, you've got eagle eyes, bro."

"Here, let me see," Neal said, taking the binoculars from him and looking. "I knew it. I thought I saw something besides an abandoned car sitting up there."

Carlos didn't hesitate to act. He turned the car around and headed south.

"Where to?"

Carlos didn't reply but instead asked, "Did you see that county road? I can't remember what it's called, but I swear we just passed it."

"Yeah, um, Keystone."

"We'll box around and see if the roads on the west are also blocked," Carlos said.

"Why wouldn't they be?" Neal questioned.

"There it is," Carlos said, turning the car hard right and accelerating.

They drove a mile and were fast approaching another major intersection.

"Looks clear," Neal said.

The flat and even desert terrain made visibility good, but if they could see, so could anyone else.

Without notice, Carlos slammed on the brakes. The huge Lincoln came to a screeching halt just at the intersection.

"You see something?" Neal asked.

"Yeah, I do," Carlos replied, his head facing left.

"What?" Neal asked as his head and eyes scanned for the possible threat.

Carlos turned the wheel hard left and slammed his foot down on the accelerator. The car lunged left and spun around until it was in the eastbound lane.

"Where are you going?" Neal exclaimed.

"I've got an idea," Carlos answered as he turned right and stopped just outside a chain-link gate.

Neal looked up and said, "Spreckels Sugar?"

"You see that?" Carlos excitedly said.

"So what?"

"You don't see what I see?" Carlos asked.

"I see a sugar high in my future, but I'm sure someone has raided this place already."

"You're right, I'm sure it has been."

"What's going through your mind, Carlos?" Neal asked.

"There's a very special ingredient you need in order to make sugar from beets," Carlos said, driving through the open gate.

"Ahh, I got it, water," Neal said, his eyebrows

raised.

"Yep, potable water, and there's a good chance others may not have thought about it. I bet they kept water in holding tanks, big ones. While we've been driving around looking for bottled water, we completely overlooked finding it in places like this," Carlos said as he drove towards the rear of the property, passing the equipment that once hummed with life. The place was a relic of a time gone by, a testament to man's ingenuity and scalable manufacturing.

While Carlos' focus was on finding the tanks, Neal's attention was on ensuring he returned home safe and alive, but mainly alive.

"Right there, I bet you that's a holding tank," Carlos said with glee. He pulled the car alongside a massive tank, the first in a row of three. The tanks were huge, standing thirty-five feet tall with a diameter of at least a hundred and twenty feet.

Not concerned with his own safety, Carlos jumped out of the car and began to race around the tank, looking for anything that would identify it as potable water.

Neal got out, but he scanned the area, looking for anything suspicious, but nothing jumped out. It was obvious that others had been to the plant, but their attention had been focused on the warehouses.

"Bingo!" Carlos hollered from the far side.

Neal made his way to Carlos and found him with his arms outstretched, attempting to hug the tank wall. Just above him was a large sign that read POTABLE WATER.

"But is there anything in them?" Neal asked.

Carlos' face scrunched, as he hadn't thought that far ahead. He raced to a small valve he had seen earlier. It was nothing more than a simple ball valve that teed off a much larger pipeline coming from the base of the tank. He turned it slowly and instantly water gushed out. Carlos cupped his hands and brought his nose to the water. "Smells fine."

Neal stepped up behind him with anticipation.

Carlos pressed his eyes closed and sipped it.

"Well?" Neal asked.

Before he opened his eyes, Carlos sang out, "It's good. Hell, it's better than good; it's the best water I've ever tasted."

Neal placed his hands under it and cupped a mouthful of water. Carlos was correct, it was good, straight from the deep aquifers that lay beneath the old desert. "There has to be more places like this. We just gave ourselves months if not years of water."

Carlos looked at each tank and said, "These have to be forty-thousand-gallon tanks. I'm not sure if they're full—heck, I bet they're not—but we have water, my friend."

"But how do we transport it back? Do we come

here daily with water jugs?" Neal asked.

"No, that's small fry. We need a tanker or a water bull that we can tow," Carlos answered.

Neal looked at the Lincoln and said, "We could use a truck too."

"That old girl can tow anything. She has a big ole V8 in her," Carlos proudly declared.

"That may be, but any significant weight on the rear end will bottom the car out."

"Shit, you're right. Well, in the meantime we'll just come here daily, fill up the biggest jugs we can find, and if we come across a running truck, we'll take it."

"We don't take anything from anyone, maybe we trade," Neal said, reminding Carlos of the pact they had made early on not to steal from others. They fully believed in salvage rights, but theft was not an option.

Carlos squinted and said, "The code, I remember."

"We have to maintain our integrity as best we can," Neal again reminded him.

"Yeah, yeah, let's fill up some jugs now and get home. We need to celebrate."

## CHAPTER FIVE

"If it were not for hopes, the heart would break." – Thomas Fuller

## Guatay, CA

The door to her eight-by-eight room creaked open, bringing in the glow of the late afternoon.

Charlotte naturally scurried towards the corner and cradled her knees to her chest in fear of who might step through.

Drew, the man who so far had offered kind words and a gentle touch, walked in and stopped two feet from her. "Hi, Charlotte."

She looked at him with her wary eyes but didn't reply to his greeting.

To appear less ominous and frightening, Drew lowered himself and squatted. "I got you something."

Charlotte looked but saw nothing.

"Do you want to see it?"

"What is it?" she asked.

"Hope told me you'd want it, so I found it," Drew said as he reached into his jacket and produced Charlotte's diary. He held it in his hand but didn't offer it to her.

Charlotte's eyes grew twice their size at the sight of it.

"I also found a pen and a pencil, not sure which you preferred," Drew said with a smile.

Charlotte sat up as tears began to flow.

Seeing this, Drew extended his arm with the diary so she could take it.

As swift as a cobra, Charlotte smacked it out of his hand. "Why, why did you take it?"

Drew recoiled from her response. "I don't understand."

"I left it at the house for my mom to find. I left it there on purpose so she'd find it and then come find us!"

"But Hope said—"

"I don't care what she said. She's a stupid little girl!"

"I was only trying to help."

Laughter erupted from the hallway beyond.

Drew craned his head and hollered, "Shut up!"

"Fucking moron!" a voice hollered back.

"Take it back, take it back and put it where you found it!" Charlotte screamed.

"I can't."

"Why not? You picked it up, now go take it back."

Drew inched closer to comfort her but was stopped when she kicked him.

"Leave me alone."

"I was only trying to help, nothing more. Hope

told me you'd want it."

"If you want to help, you'll take it back and leave it exactly where I left it."

A man came to the doorway. "Drew, enough of this good-guy bullshit."

Drew stood up and walked over to the man.

Charlotte couldn't quite make out the man Drew was talking to, but his voice was familiar. In fact, it sounded like the man her father was talking with just before being shot. She leaned to one side, but still he was obscured by the shadows.

Both men mumbled and Drew turned to walk back. The other man stood for a moment then walked away as fast as he had appeared.

Drew approached Charlotte and assumed his crouching position a few feet from her. "Charlotte, do you know why we came to your house that day?"

"To kill my dad."

"No, it wasn't like that."

"Then why?"

Drew opened his mouth, but no words came out. He deliberately paused and thought just how he'd phrase what he was about to say. "Your father, he was friends with Tony."

"Who's Tony?"

"Oh, Tony, he's my boss, the man who was just here."

Charlotte leered at him and snapped, "He was

the man who killed him."

"Yes, yes, he did, but he had good reason."

"What did my dad do to deserve being killed?"

Drew could see the anger rising in Charlotte, so he tried to stem it with something she'd want. "How about we make a deal, huh? How about you tell me something, and I'll let you see your sister, heck, I'll even make sure you two live together."

The mere mention of Hope brought Charlotte to her knees. "I want to see my sister."

"I know you do, so let's make that happen, but I need you to help me first. You help me, I'll help you."

"What do you want to know?"

"Your dad and my boss were old friends—"

Charlotte cut him off and said, "That's not true. I never saw your boss but once before that day."

Drew chuckled and said, "How about you close your mouth so I can speak? There's a lot about your father you're not aware of. Maybe he wasn't the type of friend who came over for Sunday dinners, but I can assure you they both knew each other and had a few drinks now and then together."

"But—"

This time it was Drew who silenced her. "Ssh, let me finish. Your dad was Tony's CPA; he helped Tony manage his money before all this happened. He did a good job, your dad, hell, Tony really liked him a lot, but then all this stuff happened, and just as fast as the lights went out, Tony's cache of gold went missing. Now that made Tony a bit angry, as gold became even more valuable."

"My dad didn't take it."

"You sure?"

"No, he wouldn't do that; my dad didn't steal. He was a good person," Charlotte insisted.

Drew again chuckled and said, "It seems that we always find out who people really were after they die, and I hate to break your heart, but your dad wasn't the good guy you thought he was."

"Don't talk about him that way. He was a good dad; he was a good person."

"Oh, I'm sure he was good to you and your sister, and he was really good at running the books. That's why Tony hired him."

"Shut up, just shut up."

"Do you want to see your sister or not?" Drew asked, his temperament taking a turn.

She nodded.

"Good, then tell me where your father hid the gold."

"I don't know anything about any gold."

"Are you sure?"

"My dad wouldn't steal. You're lying."

Drew stood up and stretched. "I can't squat like that anymore for any real length of time; it just cuts off the circulation." He looked at Charlotte and genuinely felt sorry for her and wanted to ensure their safety, but he wasn't sure if he could. "I'm gonna go now. If you remember anything, please call the guard and have them come get me. Will you do that?"

"When can I see my sister?"

"When you tell me where the gold is hidden," Drew replied before turning away.

"I told you I don't know where any gold is. My dad wouldn't steal."

Drew stopped at the door and turned, "Charlotte my sweet girl, you didn't really know your father, did you? He was the accountant who helped Anthony Gonzalez, one of the biggest cartel bosses in the Southwest, launder his drug money. My sweet, sweet Charlotte, your father was the man who helped Tony become legit, but before he kept the books for him, he ensured the hit men were paid and the smugglers were taken care of. I'd say your dad wasn't the good man you think he was. We all liked him, he was a funny guy, but don't mistake his tenderness with you for an inability to steal."

Charlotte's mouth hung open in shock.

"I really want to help you, I want to make sure you stay safe, but I won't be able to help you if you won't help me. Think about that," Drew said then exited the room, closing the door behind him.

## CHAPTER SIX

"When you say a situation or a person is hopeless, you are slamming the door in the face of God." – Charles L. Allen

### El Centro, CA

Like the many days before, Neal found Carlos standing next to his car. This time the dour or solemn look on his face was replaced with a jovial one.

"Good morning!" Carlos happily said.

"Good morning. Ha, look at you, all happy and raring to go," Neal said, tossing his gear into the passenger seat.

"Because it's a glorious day," Carlos said, slapping Neal on the back and jogging to the driver's seat. He slid behind the wheel and turned the car over.

Neal waited for Carlos to put the car in gear, but nothing happened.

"Everything okay?" Neal asked.

"Natalie and I had a great chat last night. We've made a decision, and I wanted to ask you. It's really important."

"So she's decided to give it up?"

"Ha, I wish, she's so damn temperamental, all

worried about getting pregnant. It also doesn't help to have her old man living in the house."

"How do you deal with that?" Neal asked, referring to the lack of intimacy. The issue had been one that had plagued Carlos for a bit, but Natalie's fear of bringing another child into this world prevented her from wanting to have sex with Carlos.

"I don't like it, but she'll come around one day. She just needs to feel safe. She does, you know, go down, so I'm taken care of, but let's not spoil what I have to share with you."

"Shoot."

"Hold on," Carlos said, turning the engine off. "No need wasting fuel."

"You okay, buddy, you look nervous as hell."

"I'm not nervous, I'm excited, I just know everything is going to be fine. I've been so uptight, but yesterday I got clarity. Finding that cache of water will help fulfill the plan I have for us, all of us."

"Okay."

"We've been thinking about where to go for some time. We know we can't stay here forever, but we've only been thinking of heading one place, south of the border. Well, you and I know it's probably a shit show down there. One place we haven't thought about is north of the border, like Canada or even Alaska. With all this water, we could make the long trek. We have the fuel stored, we have the food, but our big hurdle was water. Now we found it. Buddy, let's go to Canada."

"Canada? Alaska?"

"Dude, all the rumors we've heard say it's fine up there. Tell me one time that you've heard one person mention it negatively?"

"I don't think I've heard anyone ever speak of it. It's like two thousand miles away."

"More like twelve hundred, but the route isn't too bad. We don't have to cross through many major cities, and if we take it slow, we can be on the lookout for any government camps and steer clear of them too. I estimate we could get there in four or five days, taking it easy."

Neal rested his head back and thought. He liked the sound of Canada but liked the sound of Alaska better. "What's twelve hundred miles away?"

"Canada."

"Just the border?"

"Yeah."

"How will we get across? I bet they have the border sealed tight."

"I'm sure they do, but there has to be the odd route or old dirt road that goes from Montana right into Alberta."

"And once we're in, then what? Where do we go? Neither you nor I have friends or family there."

"We push north; maybe we do go as far as

Alaska."

Neal sat silent. The idea was the best he'd heard yet, but there was still one issue. "It has to be Alaska."

"That's fine, Alaska it is. So you're in?" Carlos asked.

"Yeah, sure, I'm in. We could be on the road for a long time. We have the food, but how will we transport the water? We need to be completely self-sufficient. We have to plan this trip as if we're not making any pit stops. We need to have everything with us," Neal stressed.

Carlos shifted in his seat and replied, "We go find ourselves a truck. I don't care if we have to steal one; we need a pickup, period."

"I won't steal from anyone. That will only bring trouble."

"Neal, you need to move past this archaic code of conduct. We need a truck. It's the truck or your family's survival."

Neal chewed on his lip and said, "I hear you, but I just believe we do things with integrity. We've done that from the beginning, and it hasn't failed us yet. If we find a truck and it's just sitting there, then we take it, but we won't be stealing it right from under the noses of its owners."

Now it was Carlos who was left chewing on his lip. He looked away at the mountains to the south and said, "Deal, no stealing from under the noses of the truck's owners." He extended his hand to Neal.

Neal took Carlos' hand and firmly shook. "You promise?"

"I promise. I wouldn't do anything that would ever hurt you, you know that."

"I know you would never do anything on purpose, but..."

"There's no buts, I promise. I'll be straight as an arrow. I've been that way since the beginning, and I'll continue to be that way."

"Good," Neal replied, liking what he heard.

Carlos let out a loud sigh and barked with excitement, "Hell yes."

"Fire it up. We have a truck to go find," Neal said.

Carlos did as he said and sped off. "Alaska, here we come, baby."

Two Miles South of Brawley, CA

Carlos leaned over the steering wheel and looked in both directions down the empty road.

Neal too was looking but more for a threat that might be waiting for them.

With it appearing all clear, Carlos pulled out of the Spreckels Sugar plant and headed east. They had just spent the past hour filling all the available water containers they could take.

"Well, we have a few more hours of light; shall we go looking for a truck?" Neal asked.

"You read my mind," Carlos replied.

"Where should we even start looking?" Neal asked.

"Good question, I thought of the farms, but I can only imagine the farmhands or migrant labor took what operational vehicles they came across and headed back south," Carlos said.

As the two talked, a white Chevrolet Suburban appeared from the *AMPM* convenient store on the corner of the intersection they were headed towards and jumped into the westbound lane.

"Jackpot!" Carlos cheered and pulled the car off onto the gravel shoulder.

Both men watched the Suburban drive past them at a high rate of speed.

Neal caught sight of two men in the front and what looked like possibly more people in the back, but it was difficult to make out with the tinted rear windows.

Carlos kept the Suburban in his sight in the side mirror, and when they were far enough away, he cranked the wheel hard to the left and slammed on the accelerator. The old Lincoln lunged hard to the left and completed the U-turn.

"Where are you going?" Neal asked, although he

knew what Carlos was doing.

"Following them."

"Why?"

Carlos raised his eyebrow and said, "That's a dumb question."

"I thought we discussed this."

"We did. I'm just seeing where they're headed. Maybe they have a spare truck."

"Bullshit. Listen, Carlos, there's no need in us looking for trouble. We've been safe since this all happened. Now we have a plan to escape this hellhole. Let's not fuck that up with anything aggressive and dumb."

"I'm not, but it's not every day we see the exact vehicle we need," Carlos replied, defending his actions.

Neal felt his heart skip a beat. This could all go badly, or it could be nothing. The thing was you didn't know until it happened.

Carlos stayed a good distance back, following each turn the Suburban made until it pulled off and headed down a long gravel driveway and stopped a hundred yards down. This was where the flat desert topography came in handy. Carlos turned left at an intersection just before the right turn down the drive and pulled into an abandoned car wash. A large grove of dead dry shrubs provided cover and concealment, but they were still able to see the

Suburban.

Neal didn't like what they were doing but had stopped fretting over it long before.

When the Lincoln came to a stop, Carlos jumped out with a set of binoculars and raced towards the thick shrubs. He put them to his eyes and focused on the Suburban that still sat idling.

Neal got out and kept his attention on everything behind and to the sides of them. If he was one thing, it was always vigilant.

"They're moving again," Carlos said, his eyes stuck to the binoculars.

"They saw us, I know it."

"You're right. I think they did, too many turns, but now they must feel safe."

A warm gust swept over them and shook the dead branches of the shrub.

"What are they doing?" Neal asked.

"Driving slowly down the road. Wait, wait a sec," Carlos muttered.

"What?" Neal asked, his gaze still focused on everything behind them. He had stayed safe for those many months and owed a lot of it to his attention to details, always following his protocol.

"Another vehicle and, guess what, it's another SUV. Hold on, make that two more," Carlos blurted out.

"Three?"

"Glad to see you can count," Carlos mused.

"Har, har."

"They're all driving north along that road," Carlos said. He focused on the road north and caught sight of a small house with several outbuildings. "I bet they're headed there."

Needing to see for himself, Neal broke from his position and walked up to Carlos. "Let me see."

Carlos handed the binoculars over without question. "Right there," he said, pointing through the bushes towards the house.

Neal peered through and saw exactly what Carlos had described. He saw all the vehicles pull up to the house, park, and what looked like a dozen people in total get out.

"Anything?" Carlos asked.

"How about making sure no one sneaks up on us?" Neal sternly said.

"We're good, so did they go to that house?"

"Yes, they've all parked and gone inside," Neal answered. He lowered the binoculars and handed them back.

"What do you think?" Carlos asked.

"I think we're wasting time. Let's get moving and try to find a truck we can use without getting into a damn battle," Neal replied, walking back to the car.

"Let's stay here a bit longer and see—"

"See what? There's nothing to see here," Neal

said.

"Who are these guys? Maybe we can find out where they got their trucks."

"From spying on them, you're going to get that? Stop the bullshit, Carlos, you're thinking about stealing one of those rigs."

Carlos opened his mouth, but no words came out.

Neal could see the devious look written all over his face. "See, I knew it."

"No, no, I wasn't."

"Yes, you were."

"Well, maybe a little. C'mon, brother, we need a fucking big rig to haul that water bull back at the plant. My old Lincoln isn't up to the task. We desperately need a truck, and lo and behold, they have them, three of them."

"Just say I agreed to your idea of stealing one, just how do you propose on getting it without getting shot up much less killed, and let me be clear, killed is the operative word."

Carlos gave Neal his signature toothy grin, tapped his index finger to his temple, and said, "With superior intellect."

## Guatay, CA

Charlotte sat frozen, her eyes stuck on the blank page of her diary. This had been her position for an hour. She didn't know what to write, and did it really matter anymore? She had asked Drew to take it back, but it appeared that wasn't going to happen.

Was there any purpose to writing? Maybe she'd find comfort in the written word, but she doubted it. How could you find comfort after everything that had happened? Her mother was missing, her father dead, and now she and her sister were captives of a drug lord—oops, reformed/turned-legit drug lord—and to add insult to it all, she found out her father worked for the man. So what could these off-white blank pages do to help?

Frustrated, she closed the diary and tossed it aside.

Her ears perked up when voices came from the other side of the door, but one voice brought her to her feet.

The door opened and there stood Hope.

"Hope!" Charlotte squealed.

Both girls ran into each other's arms.

Hope instantly began to cry.

"Are you well? Have they taken care of you? You're not hurt, are you?" Charlotte asked.

"I miss Dada," was all Hope could mutter

between the sobs.

"I miss him too," Charlotte said before asking her the all-important question, "Did they say anything about Daddy?"

Hope remained quiet.

Charlotte pulled her away so she could see her face. "Did they tell you anything about what Daddy did for work?"

Hope wiped the tears from her rosy cheeks and shook her head. "No."

"Nothing?"

"No."

"And you're fine? They haven't touched you anywhere they shouldn't?"

"No. No one touched me."

Drew stepped into the room and stood with a large smile on his face. "Hi, girls."

Charlotte pulled Hope close and took a couple steps away from him.

He chuckled and said, "You still don't trust me? If I was going to bite, I would've bitten. But I wanted to show I was a man of my word. I promised I'd let you see your sister if you told me the truth."

"So you believed me?" Charlotte asked, clearly confused, especially after his reaction the last time.

Drew ran his fingers through his thick black hair and said, "I'll have to admit, I didn't believe you, but something came up, and well, we now know you were being honest."

"You found it?" Charlotte asked.

Hope just stood with most of her weight against Charlotte.

"We're going to get it now."

"Who had it? Did my...?"

"No, no. Unfortunately it was someone else in our crew. We had our suspicions and they were well founded. I'm disappointed, but it is what it is."

"You'll let us go?" Charlotte asked.

"Sorry, but that's not going to happen."

"But you found the gold."

Drew walked up to them and said, "We have another plan for you two."

"What?" Charlotte asked, her lips trembling.

He looked down, his face strained as veins popped on his neck and forehead. "You girls are valuable, you're assets, and we intend on selling you to a slaver in Mexico."

"You can't, no!" Charlotte screamed.

"I'm sorry, but it's not my call. I'm just the messenger."

Hope began crying again. She had heard of the word slave, but she couldn't quite comprehend what it meant. Her tears emanated from fear.

"No, no, you can't!" Charlotte screamed.

Drew stepped closer so he could impart something quietly, but his approach was repelled.

"Get away from us!" Charlotte yelled as she hit him with her fist.

He withdrew but was more sad than angry. "I'm sorry, it's not my call. I promise if it were up to me, you'd stay with us."

"What's to come of us?"

"I'll make sure we sell you together, okay?" Drew said in a weak attempt at comforting her.

"Leave us alone, go, go!" Charlotte demanded.

"Let me talk to the boss again, see what I can do," Drew said, again trying to make them feel at ease.

"Go!"

Nervously Drew exited but not before he said, "I'll have dinner dropped off with an extra set of blankets for Hope. She can stay with you."

The door closed and locked.

"What's going to happen to us?" Hope asked.

Charlotte hugged Hope tightly and repeated the exact words her father would say when she was scared. "It will be fine. I'll keep you safe."

Hope looked up at Charlotte and cried, "It won't be fine."

El Centro, CA

Neal stormed into the house and slammed the door. "God, he frustrates me sometimes!"

Karen rushed into the living room and asked, "What, what's going on?"

"Carlos, he can be a stubborn fool."

"What happened?"

Neal shrugged, looked at Karen, and remembered that it was his job to remain calm, cool and collected.

Karen cleared the few feet separating them and asked, "Tell me what happened?"

Beth ran in with her arms open wide. "Daddy!" She jumped in his open embrace.

"Hi, sweetie," Neal said to Beth as he gave her several kisses on her cheeks and forehead. Her presence alone calmed him.

"I missed you," Beth said, her arms draped around his neck.

Karen wrapped her arms around both of them and said, "I missed you too, Daddy." She and Neal had agreed to keep disagreements and anything that could disrupt the house to a minimum. "We'll talk later."

"Good plan, it's been a big day. I have a lot to share with you," Neal said.

"Come on in, get undressed, and relax a bit," Karen said, removing his vest. "I'll have dinner ready soon."

"I can't. I have first shift," Neal said, referring to the watch shifts he and Carlos rotated every eight hours when they were back at home.

"Then we'll join you, and you can tell me all the news," Karen said.

Neal rubbed his sore neck before proceeding to the spare bedroom. There he had a chair positioned next to a large window with a good vantage point of the street and houses beyond.

Minutes passed before Karen came in with a plate of warm pasta.

Neal looked at the food, smiled and said, "Yum, Chef Boyardee raviolis."

"Bethie wanted it, but I can make you something else."

"No, it's fine," Neal said, stabbing his fork into one of the plump raviolis.

"You ready to talk?" Karen asked.

Neal looked past her and asked, "Where's Beth?"

"In her room, coloring."

He set the plate down and relaxed into the chair. "Carlos and I have made initial plans on relocating."

The news gave Karen pause. "Relocating?"

"We can't live here forever. Eventually we'll run out of food, but water is the main issue, and we have to come to grips with living in a desert. The water will soon run dry."

"But you found a large supply, enough to last—"

Neal cut her off. "Enough to last months maybe; that's if someone else doesn't find it."

"But you said—"

"I know this might be hard to fathom because we've been surviving so well for a long time, but it can't last, it won't. We have to make a run for it; we have to go to a safe zone."

"I'm not going to a FEMA camp."

"Oh God, Karen, I'd never do that. No, no, no, you're misunderstanding me. We're going to make a push for Alaska. We feel confident it's safe there."

"You don't know if it is or not," Karen said, her voice cracking.

Neal sighed; he hated having these conversations with Karen. "Karen, we have to take a chance, we have to."

"But maybe you'll find more water. Maybe all we need to do is keep making do here and things will go back to normal."

He took her hand and rubbed it. "Sweetheart, nothing is going back to normal."

"You don't know that, just like you don't know if Alaska is safe. For all you know, it could be just like this."

"That's true. I don't know for sure. I could be wrong, but what I do know is we'll run out of water, it's only a matter of time, then what? We have all the food and water we need right now to make a push north. I can't risk using up our resources then going. We don't know how long we'll be on the road."

"So you and Carlos make up your minds, and we're just supposed to go along?" Karen asked mockingly.

Neal's eyes widened upon hearing that. Karen wasn't one to aggressively challenge him when it pertained to these matters. He knew that it stemmed from her fear and not a confidence in his ability to make clear and sound decisions. "Karen, what's wrong?"

"This is wrong, this idea of yours. It's risky, too risky. Neal, you've been telling me almost daily how bad it is out there, and now you want to put us, your family, right in the middle of it for days, maybe weeks?" She pulled her hand away and folded her arms.

"We can't stay here forever, we just can't. You know how the summers are."

Flustered, she began pacing the room.

"Karen, we will plan a route that keeps us away from all major cities. We'll travel during the day and camp at night, off road. I won't do anything without ensuring it's well thought out."

"What about the boat? What about getting us all to the boat in San Diego and sailing somewhere like Hawaii or Costa Rica? We loved Costa Rica."

"We've talked about this; the big cities are no-go zones. I've heard the gangs have taken over; plus we don't even know if the boat's there anymore."

Her pacing stopped.

He turned around to see her looking out a side window. He then heard her crying. He jumped up and raced to her. "Why are you crying?"

Wiping away the tears, she explained, "I'm just thinking about my sister."

He didn't know what to say; it had been a topic since day one. Karen's sister, Kate, lived just outside of New York City, and they hadn't heard from her since before the day it all went dark.

"I've said it before; I'll go looking for her if you want?"

Karen reached for his hand and grasped it. Looking down at his open hand, she ran her thumb over the thick calluses. "You're a hard worker, always have been."

He was speechless watching her.

"You'd do anything if I asked, I know that. If I asked you to go look for her, you'd do it in a second. I know you. But it's not worth losing you. Is that wrong? Am I being selfish? I don't want to lose you, we need you, but I also would like to know if she's fine. But New York is so far away. It would be an impossible trip, too risky. I have to come to grips with probably not seeing my sister again."

"I hate that you have to feel that way."

Several tears fell from her chin and landed in his open palm. "It's just the way things are. It is what it is."

"She's family," Neal said.

"She is, but you and Beth are really my *family*. When we married, I left that family and joined with you. Together we created this, we created Beth."

He lifted her head up gently and asked, "I've asked before and I'll ask again, do you want me to go find your sister?"

"I feel awful, but no, and don't ask me again. My tears are for the world that's gone; the possibilities of that world are lost to us now. I just wonder what happened to her. I pray she's fine, but I just don't know. I feel deep down she's still alive."

"You do?"

"Yeah, I think I'd know if she had left this world."

"I just want us to be safe; I want nothing else more than that."

"Oh, honey, I know that, I trust you. I'm…I'm just scared. You know me, I like certainty, and going on the road, going out there is so uncertain. If it were just you and me, I'd say let's go, but it's not just us. I fear for little Bethie."

"That's totally understandable, and if I thought us staying here was better in the long run, I'd stay, but it's not. We can't stay here forever, we just can't."

She spun around, wrapped her arms around his muscular build, and rested her head on his shoulder.

"I love you," he said.

"I know you do."

"Gross!" Beth squealed loudly from the doorway.

"Come here, sweetie," Karen said.

Beth rushed in and sandwiched herself in between them. "What's going on?"

"We were just talking," Neal replied.

"Adult stuff?" Beth asked.

Karen knelt down, looked Beth in the eyes, and asked, "How would you like to go on a road trip?"

"We're leaving?" Beth asked.

Neal cracked a slight smile. This was Karen's way of giving her answer.

"Alaska, we're going to Alaska."

"Aren't there polar bears up there?" Beth asked.

"Not the part we're going to, but yes, I guess you could find some in the most northern regions," Neal answered.

"Can I bring my toys?"

Her question brought tears to his eyes. Even after all that had happened, she had maintained an innocence that only children could have. He loved her for that and wanted her to remain that way for as long as possible.

Neal shot up from a dead sleep and looked around. The intense black of night made it impossible to see.

He reached for the flashlight on his nightstand, but hesitated to turn it on for fear of giving himself away. With his right hand he picked up the pistol and held it firmly.

"Neal?" Karen asked.

"Ssh."

His response jolted her from blissful slumber to concern. She too tried to see in the dark but to no avail.

Under her breath she whispered, "Turn on the flashlight."

"Ssh," he again said but more forcefully this time. He exited the bedroom and stood in the hallway, allowing his ears to try to hear anything.

A loud knock at the front door jolted him.

He cruised stealthily through the house until his back was against the wall next to the front door.

More loud knocking followed by a familiar voice. "Neal, Neal, open up."

It was Natalie and she sounded scared.

Neal unlocked the two deadbolts and removed the custom-made door jam. When he opened the door fully, he found Natalie standing alone.

She rushed past him into the house. "Neal, you need to stop him."

"Stop who?" Neal asked. He clicked on the flashlight so he could see her more clearly.

"He was talking crazy, saying he needed to go,

go by himself. Neal, you need to stop him. He just left; he can't be far."

"Natalie, calm down. What are you talking about?" Neal said.

The glow of the flashlight lit the room and cast long shadows on the wall.

"I told him not to go, but he waited until we were all asleep. He snuck out."

"Do you know where Ricky would have gone?" Neal asked, assuming the person she was talking about was her son.

"Ricky? No, Carlos, it's Carlos. He kept talking about this truck and that he needed to go get it by himself because you wouldn't go."

"Oh no."

Karen rushed into the room and darted for Natalie. She put her arm around her and said, "Neal will find him."

"I, um," Neal mumbled.

Karen glared and said, "You'll go out and bring him back."

"I don't know if that's a good idea," Neal countered.

"He was acting weird, manic in some way. I guess you two got in an argument about it," Natalie said.

"You have to go," Karen insisted.

"It's not safe," Neal countered.

"I'm scared. I'm really worried about him. Why would he leave in the middle of the night, just go. What's he thinking?" Natalie asked.

Karen left Natalie's side and stepped up to Neal.

"What truck?"

"I never got a chance to talk to you about it. It was why I was upset when I came home."

"What truck?" Karen again asked.

Neal explained to them both what happened but from his perspective that attempting to steal the truck was foolhardy.

"Neal, you have to go stop him," Karen pressed.

Neal stood, his arms folded, contemplating what he should do but fully knowing Carlos was miles ahead of him, and without knowing just how he planned on stealing the truck, any approach by him could jeopardize both of them. He expressed these concerns.

"So what do we do? Just wait and pray?" Natalie asked.

"I can go right now, but there's no chance I'll beat him there, and if I show up, I can screw up whatever plan he had. I think we need to let this play out," Neal said.

"Maybe you can go talk to these men," Karen said.

"Not a good idea."

"You have to do something," Natalie said.

"Yes, you have to do something," Karen echoed.

Neal's temper was flaring because he knew he wasn't going to be able to reason with the women. Frustrated, he walked off and headed towards the spare room.

"Where are you going?" Karen asked.

Neal didn't stop or turn to reply. He kept walking and said, "I am going to do something. I'm gonna take watch, and while I'm waiting, I'll pray Carlos comes home safely."

Neal lost count of how many times Karen and Natalie came in asking him to go find Carlos. At first they were righteous and almost indignant, but after a while their attitude shifted to pleas, but it wasn't enough for him to move. He had a mixed range of emotions coursing through him. The shock quickly wore off and was replaced by anger; the anger eventually shifted to disappointment then to worry. Regardless of how many times they asked, Neal stuck to his guns and refused to go out. He knew doing so put him, Carlos and everyone there at risk. If something bad happened to Carlos, Neal was still alive to help, but if they both didn't return, what would happen to Karen and Beth? Neal just couldn't find it in him to go out. If Carlos made this haphazard decision, he'd have to complete it all alone.

The women eventually quit asking and soon

thereafter fell asleep on the couch.

Neal fought the urge to close his eyes, but when the dim light of dawn came, the fatigue vanished along with the darkness. He stretched, rubbed his eyes, and vigorously paced the small room. He stopped when he heard a deep throttled rumble in the distance.

Could that be? he asked himself as he leaned close to the open window and listened.

Tires squealed and again a deep rumble echoed off the houses in the distance but now closer. The sound drew closer and closer until he was sure it was heading towards them. Excited, he grabbed his rifle, tore out of the room, and stepped outside on the front steps to listen.

Whoever it was could be heard on his street now.

Always a man who took precautions, Neal raised his rifle and placed it against his shoulder. Out of the corner of his eyes, he spotted a Suburban similar to the one he had seen yesterday.

The Suburban drove into the cul-de-sac and stopped feet from Carlos' driveway.

Neal couldn't make out the driver through the darkly tinted glass, but he guessed it was Carlos returning victoriously.

Karen and Natalie had also heard the Suburban and came outside.

"Is it Carlos?" Natalie asked.

"Stay put. I don't know for sure," Neal said, stepping off the steps and slowly advancing towards the driver's side of the vehicle.

The driver's door opened up.

Neal looked through his sights and placed his index finger on the trigger.

Carlos emerged, but something was wrong.

Seeing Carlos, Neal lowered the rifle and raced towards him.

Carlos raised his hand, smiled and said, "I told you." He lowered his arm then fell hard to his knees.

Natalie screamed and bolted towards Carlos with Karen just behind her.

Neal reached Carlos just before he fell over. "I got you, buddy."

"I told you, I fucking told you," Carlos said proudly.

Neal's hand felt warm and wet. He looked down and saw it was red with blood. "You're hurt."

Carlos coughed and replied, "Um, yeah, I got shot."

Natalie fell to her knees and began kissing Carlos on the forehead. "You stupid, stupid man, why, why?"

"I'm good, baby," Carlos said. By his temperament, he wasn't feeling too much pain and was actually quite happy about his success.

"Let's take you inside and get you patched up," Neal said, bringing Carlos to his feet. "Can you walk?"

"Yeah, let me just hold on to you," Carlos answered.

With Carlos clinging to him, Neal slowly walked inside Carlos' house and towards the spare bedroom in the back of the house.

Natalie frantically cleared the spare bed. "Put him right here."

Neal put him in the bed and asked, "Where are you hurt?"

"My left side, just above my hip," Carlos replied, pulling at his shirt.

The T-shirt Carlos was wearing was soaked with blood. Neal pulled it up and easily found the bullet wound. He examined it and said, "Clean shot, in and out, looks like it just went through some muscle. You're one lucky son of a bitch."

Carlos chuckled and said, "I'll tell you what, it didn't hurt at first, but once my adrenaline wore off, it hurt real bad. Thank God I had that syringe of morphine."

"You shot up morphine?" Neal asked as he cleaned the wound with a clean cloth.

Karen suddenly appeared with the trauma kit. "Here, you'll need this."

Carlos ignored Karen and answered Neal's

question, "Yeah, remember we found them months ago?"

"I remember," Neal said, his full attention on the wound.

"Well, they came in handy. I only used a quarter of the syringe. That shit works great; I can see how people can get addicted."

With the wound completely clean, Neal got an even better look. His previous assessment proved accurate. The bullet had traveled from his lower back straight through and out the front; the damage was limited to tissue only.

"Where's the Lincoln?" Neal asked.

"I hid it over at the strip mall," Carlos said, referring to the small strip mall where they had parked the day before.

"Well, when you're healed up, we'll go get it."

Carlos grabbed Neal's forearm and squeezed. "I told you, I told you I'd get the fucking truck. I fucking told you."

With a half grin, Neal said, "You were right, you got it. I just hope you're right in the end."

"What the hell does that mean?" Carlos asked, grimacing.

"I just hope you're right and this doesn't come back to haunt us."

## CHAPTER SEVEN

"While it is important for people to see your promise you must also remember that hope is the keeper of both happiness and disappointment, the father of both progress and failure." – Bryant H. McGill

Guatay, CA

Charlotte looked up at the deep blue sky. It was so good to see it. The fresh air added to the rare experience and brought a smile to her face.

Hope ran up holding a teddy bear. "Look what Drew gave me. Isn't he cute? I think I'll call him Cuddles."

"Cute," Charlotte said smugly.

It had been a couple days since Hope and she had been reunited. No word had come about their being sold, but knowing it was still unresolved hung over Charlotte like a dark cloud.

Hope's sense of perspective seemed to be short as she settled in more and more. It helped that Drew kept showing up with gifts, sweets, and what could only be described as tenderness in his approach to them.

After enjoying her respite from the dark room, Charlotte began to assess where she was. She turned around and looked at the building she and Hope had called home and noticed it was a large metal barn. To either side of it sat two smaller structures made from the same material. Across from the barn, a large two-story house sat surrounded by large pine trees. To the left of it sat a large detached six-bay garage. Men came and went from the garage and house. She counted eleven men, none of whom she recalled seeing before. To the left of the garage, a long and narrow gravel driveway winded down towards a massive metal gate and was guarded by two armed men. That brought the number to thirteen and didn't count Drew and Tony. From the gate she took note of the tall chain-link fence that extended out from either side. She followed one side and saw it disappeared behind a hillside; she followed the other side until it too vanished. Behind the barn a large tree-covered rocky hill towered over them. She couldn't see any other house or building outside the fence line.

"Girls!" Drew hollered as he exited the house, his arms high in the air.

"Hi, Drew!" Hope replied.

Charlotte nudged Hope out of irritation. How could she respond to him so happily? It was as if she had forgotten everything that had happened.

Drew strutted over and gave Hope a hug. "How's my little friend doing?"

"Good," Hope answered.

"And you, how's the big sister today?" Drew asked.

Charlotte was stubborn and decided to ignore him.

He smiled and said, "You're a tough nut to crack, aren't you?"

Charlotte cocked her head and smirked. "Are you serious?"

"I'm doing my best; plus I have some good news and some bad news," Drew said.

Hope cradled her teddy bear and began to play make-believe with it.

"So which is it first?"

"You're gross," Charlotte shot back.

"Since you're in a sour mood, I'll go with the bad news. You both are stuck with me."

Charlotte folded her arms, disgusted by Drew and his attempt to be fun. Her only reply to him was a rolling of her eyes.

"Now for the good news."

"Yeah, I like good news," Hope said to Cuddles.

"Hope, you have a positive attitude; you're going to go far," Drew said, patting Hope on the top of her head.

"She's a six-year-old, what do you expect?" Charlotte barked.

"I'm six and a half," Hope said.

"Whatever," Charlotte grumbled.

"Charlotte, I know you're upset. You have every right to be angry, but your situation is your situation. I can only tell you to make the most of it."

"How am I to make the most of it? My life sucks! My mom is missing, you killed my dad, and we're to be sold off as fucking slaves."

Hope's eyes grew as big as saucers.

Drew planted his hands on his hips. He wanted to counter her anger, but he knew she needed to vent.

"Tell me, please tell me how I'm supposed to make the most of this shit show?"

"You said another bad word," Hope said, astonished. She hadn't heard Charlotte speak this way before.

"Oh, shut up and play with your teddy bear," Charlotte barked. She turned and headed towards a bench she had seen earlier next to a grouping of trees.

"C'mon, I have some good news," Drew shouted.

Ignoring him, she treaded on.

Drew wanted to tell her and wasn't giving up that easy. "Hey, walk with me so I can tell your sister the good news," he said to Hope. He held out his hand, but Hope just stared. She had been accepting of his help, but here was where she drew the line. Seeing that she wasn't going to take his hand, he awkwardly retracted it and again asked, "You want to hear the good news?"

Hope nodded.

"Then follow me," Drew said and marched towards Charlotte.

"Leave me alone," Charlotte barked, glaring intensely at Drew.

"I need to tell you something important," Drew insisted.

Laughter erupted from a small group of men that had gathered near the garage.

Charlotte and Drew looked and saw them pointing at them.

"What are they laughing at?" Charlotte asked.

"It's nothing. Ignore them," Drew said.

Charlotte had given up on being nice. If she was going to be sold off, she just didn't care anymore. She lifted her hand and raised her middle finger at them.

Seeing her response, the men roared even louder with laughter.

"Put your hand down," Drew ordered.

Hope shuffled over and sat next to Charlotte on the old wooden bench.

"Christ, between you and those idiots over there, it's impossible for me to tell you that I secured your freedom."

Charlotte's face instantly changed from anger to

shock. "What?"

"That's the good news. You won't be sold."

"You're letting us go?" Charlotte asked.

"We can go home now?" Hope asked.

"No, you can't; that was the bad news," Drew said. His face twisted as he thought about the best way to tell them the next bit.

"You said the bad news was we were stuck with you. What does that mean?" Charlotte asked.

"I did everything I could, I talked Tony's ear off, but he wouldn't budge. He's a good guy, well, maybe not a good guy, but he does have a heart in some ways. Anyway, he looks at you guys as a business transaction, nothing more, so I couldn't persuade him with sympathy, so I had to buy you."

"What?" Charlotte snapped. Her mouth gaped open.

"There wasn't any other way. He wouldn't let you go unless I paid the amount he was seeking from the slavers," Drew said.

"I don't understand, what does that mean? You own us?" Charlotte asked, her face flush with anger.

"Technically yes, but I won't do anything to hurt you, I swear," Drew insisted.

"I want to go home," Hope said.

"You're crazy. You're all crazy, cruel and mean," Charlotte yelled.

The men again roared with laughter and began to

mock Drew.

"Fuck off!" Drew hollered then turned his attention back to the girls. "You need to know that after everything blows over, I intend on letting you go home, but right now it's too dangerous out there."

"We were fine until you showed up," Charlotte said.

"If it wasn't us, it was bound to be someone else," Drew replied.

"That's not true and you know it. If you care about us, then you'll return us home," Charlotte barked.

The group of men had grown, and the larger they got, the louder they became, their laughter echoing off the buildings.

Drew's patience with Charlotte was running thin. It didn't help that he was also being ridiculed. Frustrated by the cackles and howls, he turned and again blasted them, "Shut the fuck up!"

"No, fuck you!" one man yelled back.

"No, fuck you," Drew yelled.

The man broke from the group and began to briskly march towards them. He was large, standing around six foot five. His arms were massive, like legs sticking out of his torso. The bright sun glimmered off his smooth bald head.

Drew turned to confront him but was clearly unnerved by his approach. "Charlie, back the fuck off."

"No, fuck you, you little mouthy bitch," Charlie hollered as he closed in on Drew and the girls.

Hope slid close to Charlotte and hid her face.

Charlie walked to within mere inches of Drew's face and stared down. "You think just because the boss has you doing his errands that you're something special. Let me give you the four-one-one, motherfucker, you're not special. The boys think you're a bitch, and you need to be taught a lesson."

"Just step back before something happens that you regret," Drew declared, standing his ground. His heart raced with anticipation of a fight he would surely lose.

"Me and the boys think I should kick your ass then take that pretty little tweenie there and teach her the benefits of womanhood."

"You have three seconds to back off," Drew said.

"The boss doesn't have a problem with us settling differences, so I say we settle this the only way—"

Drew counted the seconds in his head. He had to act because he knew what Charlie meant about settling differences, and he wasn't about to wait for Charlie to make it official. He swiftly swung up with his right fist and drove it under Charlie's jaw. The blow was fast and powerful.

Charlie didn't see it coming and wasn't expecting it. He had underestimated Drew and at his own cost. The powerful undercut rattled his jaw and sent him reeling backwards.

As Charlie wobbled, trying to get his footing, Drew struck again, this time coming down with his right fist. He connected against the left side of Charlie's face near the point where his jaw hinged. This second blow was successful.

Charlie's already wobbly legs gave out, and he dropped to the ground hard.

Drew wasn't finished. He couldn't allow Charlie to rise; plus he needed to prove not only to Charlie but to the men watching that he wasn't someone to be messed with. He straddled Charlie's unconscious body and leveled one heavy punch after another.

Witnessing the vicious attack stunned Charlotte.

Hope quivered as she heard the fight; she was too scared to look.

Drew didn't know how many times he had hit Charlie before being pulled off by several men.

"Stop," one man said.

"You're going to kill him," another said.

Drew struggled to get free. He was enraged and wanted to keep punishing Charlie. "Let me go."

A single gunshot cracked.

Everyone froze.

"Enough!" Tony hollered from the front of the

house, his pistol raised over his head.

Drew shrugged off the men and looked towards Tony before assessing the damage he had inflicted on Charlie.

Tony strode over. He looked down at Charlie and shook his head. "What the fuck is going on?"

"Charlie was mouthing off, and well, it was going towards violence, so I went ahead—"

"I've heard enough," Tony said, waving his hand at Drew. "What did you see?" Tony asked the men.

"Um, Charlie here was making fun of Drew and the girls. Um, anyway, you see, ahh, they, them two began yelling at each other. Ahh, Charlie came over, and before you know it, Drew here was kicking his ass."

"Is that what you saw?" Tony asked a second man.

"Yes, sir."

"Okay, so you guys decided to settle your differences, and by the looks of Charlie, the matter is settled, correct?" Tony said.

Everyone, including Drew, nodded in agreement.

"Good, now get Charlie to the doc," Tony ordered.

Two men carried Charlie's bloody and battered body away.

Tony cracked his neck, a bad habit he often did before lecturing or admonishing people. He looked at Drew and said, "D, what the fuck? Did you have to beat him so badly? Huh? Charlie's a good guy, a bit rough and foulmouthed, but he's a good part of our team. Look at what you did, you busted him up real bad."

Drew watched as Charlie was carried away. He heard what Tony was saying but didn't care much about what he had done to Charlie; what he was concerned about was Tony's reaction. "Sorry, boss."

"Sorry, boss? That's it? I let you buy these little brats because you're a fucking bleeding heart, then you go and wreck one of my men, a valuable part of our team," Tony said.

"I was afraid he'd kill me. You and I both know what Charlie's capable of," Drew said in his defense.

"Yeah, I know, but did you have to get on top of him and pound his head in?"

Drew looked at his bloody hands and bruised knuckles but didn't answer.

Tony shoved Drew. "I asked you a question."

"No, boss, I shouldn't have done that."

Tony looked at the girls and smirked. "I don't get you, I just don't. One second I think you're becoming a split tail, then you go all Rocky on Charlie." He reached out, pinched Drew's cheek then patted it. "Make sure you're thinking clearly, okay? I think these little brats have got your head all messed up."

"Yes, boss."

"Good, now go get cleaned up and keep those little brats inside. You know the men get all weird," Tony said and walked away.

Drew looked at Charlotte and Hope and said, "Best you go inside."

Charlotte didn't hesitate. She nudged Hope, and the two got up right away and hurried towards the barn. As she walked with Hope, Charlotte made up her mind that she needed to escape. She was unsure just how she'd do it, but staying there was not an option.

## El Centro, CA

Neal walked into the kitchen, hoping to find a snack, but instead found Karen packing a cardboard box with canned food. He smiled and stepped up behind her. "You're so sweet."

"It's not a matter of being sweet, it's the right thing to do," she replied as she kept loading the box.

The box was a gift for Felicia, an elderly lady who lived alone in a house several blocks away. They had offered her a place with them, but she insisted on staying in the house she and her long-since-deceased husband had first purchased decades ago.

Karen had taken Felicia under her care and every week would take her food and check in on her.

Neal rubbed her shoulders and sighed.

She stopped and turned. "I know you're mad at Carlos, but what's done is done."

"It's not that."

"What is it?"

"I'm ashamed of myself," Neal confessed.

"Why?"

"Because I should have done something. I sat around while Carlos was out there getting shot."

"You did what you thought was best."

"But you told me to go, hell, you begged me to go, but I didn't."

"It is what it is."

Neal looked down and shook his head. "I was afraid."

Seeing the inner turmoil he was feeling, Karen caressed his arm. "I'm sure you were."

"Not for me, not like that. I'm afraid of something happening to me."

"That makes—"

He interrupted her by placing his finger on her lips. "Let me finish. I'm afraid for you and Beth. If I die, what will happen to you? It terrifies me to the point of inaction. That's what happened. I was afraid to go out not because I was fearful of my own death, I'm fearful for yours."

"I can appreciate that, I can, but you have to trust us. Me and Bethie are tougher than you think."

"I know, it just plagues my mind," Neal continued.

"Sweetheart, I want you to know that I love and trust you. We've made it this far, and I know in my heart we'll make it all the way to Alaska or wherever we end up," she softly and reassuringly said. "Now let me finish packing up these things for Felicia."

"Let me help you," Neal said.

"You want to come with us?" Karen asked.

"Sure, that will be great. It's been a while since I've seen that crazy old lady," Neal jested.

Karen elbowed him in the side and said, "She's not crazy…she's unique."

"You call her unique, but that's just another word for crazy."

"I like her a lot. She's a bit flighty, but I hope I'm as lucid as she is when I'm eighty-two."

"Birds of a feather."

"Huh?"

"Ahh, nothing," he quipped.

"Are you saying I'm crazy?" she asked, placing her hand on her hip as she squinted and leered at him.

"Nope, not at all," he joked.

She punched him in the arm and went back to packing.

Beth loved the short walk to Felicia's house.

Anything to get out and see the world beyond the four walls of their house made her happy. She skipped and sang as they went.

Neal pulled Beth's overloaded Red Rider wagon, which towered with boxes and water. He smiled broadly as he watched Beth sing happily. Seeing her so joyful filled him with bliss, which temporarily kept his concerns about their pending trip at bay.

Soon they'd be on the road and heading north. With the truck in their possession, there wasn't anything that would stop them now.

While Carlos healed, they'd plan and pack.

Karen, though, had her mind on Felicia. What would become of her?

"I'm going to ask Felicia to come with us," Karen said.

"That's fine. I just don't see her budging," Neal replied.

"I'll convince her. If she doesn't, she'll die, you know that."

"I think she should come with us, but I don't see her doing it."

Karen stopped him. They were now feet away from her front door. "Don't be so cavalier about this."

"I'm not. I just know she won't go," Neal said and pointed at the house. "You see this place? This is her home. Her husband's ashes sit on the mantel. She raised a child in this old home; she doesn't know anything else. The only way she'd leave is if we kidnap her."

"Then we kidnap her."

"You're joking."

"We can't just leave her."

"I'm not saying we leave her, but we need to let her do what she wants to do. We can't force anybody to do anything."

"You're right, but we have to try."

"And try we will."

"Good, I just wanted to make sure we were thinking the same."

"We are. Now can we go in?"

They continued down the sidewalk.

"You know what I'm craving right now? Those jarred peaches, did you see those?" Neal asked, referencing a crate of homemade canned peaches that were found in the back of the Suburban.

"I saw them, and I packed a jar for Felicia."

"That will be a nice surprise," Neal said just as he knocked.

The door swung open immediately.

"Well, hello, hello," Felicia said, opening the screen door that separated them. "Come in, please come in."

Neal was always impressed when he saw Felicia. She was so small and frail, but there was a spirit to her that made her seem powerful. She stood just over five feet and must have weighed a little more than a hundred pounds, but it never stopped her.

As Neal hauled the boxes in, Felicia cleared the chairs in her dining nook so everyone could sit down. "Sorry, I've been going through photos. I was never one to scrapbook, but now seemed like a good time."

Hearing her say this broke Karen's heart. She knew Felicia was alone. The one child she had lived in Florida and had become estranged over the years. For all intents and purposes, Karen, Neal and Beth were her family.

Beth went directly to the makeshift playroom Felicia had created for her months ago. There she played with toys like Lincoln Logs, Hot Wheels and even a Howdy Doody doll. Neal joked that all the toys were older than him.

Excited to show Felicia the peaches, Karen pulled them from the box Neal was carrying. "Look what we have for you, Felicia."

Felicia came in from the kitchen, squinting, and asked, "What, dear?"

"Peaches, canned peaches."

"Oh my, I haven't had peaches in ages. Let's open them up," Felicia said, excited about all the goodies but especially the peaches.

Karen and Felicia disappeared into the kitchen, leaving Neal to unload everything. One by one he brought the boxes and cases of water inside.

"Daddy, something smells bad," Beth said as she pointed down the hallway.

"Where?"

Beth just pointed.

Neal put the box down and headed down the hallway. Within a few steps a strong fecal odor hit him. He remembered where the powder room was and opened it to discover the toilet had overflowed. He saw that she had removed the cover he had placed on it. Disgusted, he closed the door and walked into the kitchen. There he found the women enjoying the jar of peaches.

"Oh my God, they're so good," Felicia cooed.

Karen took a large piece between her fingers and dropped it into her mouth. When she saw Neal, she excitedly grabbed another piece and said, "Sweetie, have one. They're great."

He was tempted but wasn't in the mood after having been in the bathroom. "Sorry, not right now," he said, then turned his attention to Felicia. "Did you remove the toilet cover in the bathroom?"

"Yes, I thought by now it would be okay to use it; plus I just got tired of going outside in that dirty latrine you dug," Felicia said with a tinge of guilt.

"You have a mess now in the bathroom," Neal admonished.

She sheepishly looked at him and said, "Sorry, I

thought it would be fine."

"Well, it's not."

"Ease up, Neal," Karen snapped.

"Fine, I'll ease up, but I'm not cleaning it up," Neal said and walked out of the room.

Beth ran by him and into the kitchen. "Yummy, peaches."

Neal was irritated, but he knew that emotion didn't originate with Felicia but was an accumulation of everything. He stepped outside and sat on the steps.

Beth came outside with a small bowl of peaches and sat next to him. "You want some?"

"Nah."

"They're yummy. Try one, please," she insisted.

"Sorry, honey, I'm not hungry."

"Oh, come on."

"Beth, are you happy?" he asked. It was a question out of left field, but he wanted to know how she felt. He wasn't sure if she'd answer honestly, but for some reason he needed to know.

"Yes," she said, her mouth full of peaches.

"Are you scared?"

"Um, no."

"Ever?"

"Sometimes, but mostly I feel fine."

"Good."

"Oops," she said, looking at the empty bowl.

"You ate them all. I thought you were saving me one," he teased.

"Sorry."

"I'm just messing around," he replied and dipped his finger in the juice and licked it. "Tastes good."

Several loud cracks of gunfire sounded in the distance.

He craned his head to listen and get the exact location.

Silence.

Nervous, he stood up.

"Daddy…"

"Go inside," he ordered.

"Why?"

A volley of gunfire cracked and popped in the direction of his house.

"Go, now!" he barked.

Beth dropped the bowl and ran inside. "Mommy, Mommy!"

Neal grabbed his rifle next to the front door and took off for his house.

Random gunshots continued then stopped as suddenly as they had started.

Neal sprinted the first two blocks. When he made the left turn onto his street, he could see the Lincoln and another SUV parked in the cul-de-sac with several men lying on the ground around the vehicles. Knowing what had happened, he increased his pace.

The scream of a woman followed by several shots came from Carlos' house.

Neal didn't need to see who screamed; he knew who it was.

Two men exited the front door. The second man was laughing while the first looked angry.

Close to the SUV, Neal took cover behind it just in time to avoid being seen. Sweat streamed down his face and his heart felt like it was going to explode. He had stayed in relatively decent shape, but that sprint had taken a lot out of him.

"Fuck," the first man cursed.

"At least we got our truck back," the second man said, patting the other on the back.

"Stay put while I look around," the first man said.

"I'll be right here, enjoying this whiskey," the other man said, sitting down on the steps. He lifted a bottle of Jim Beam and took a sip.

Neal peered around the side of the SUV to get his bearings. He saw the man sitting but had lost sight of the first man. "Where did you go?"

The first man exited not a second later and said, "You gotta see the stash this motherfucker had."

"I wish you hadn't killed that tight piece of ass. I could've gone for getting my dick wet today," the second disgustingly joked then took a swig of whiskey.

"That bitch bit me; she had it coming. And that little fucking kid, did you see his head explode?"

Neal heard the entire conversation, and it left his blood boiling. He had enough; he couldn't stand and listen to these animals anymore. With his thumb he flipped off the selector switch on the M4 and pivoted away from the SUV. He was exposed, but he also had a clear shot. It wasn't the most tactical thing to do, but right now he was running on anger.

By the time the men saw him, Neal had fired several shots.

Those shots hit the man on the stairs squarely in the chest. He reeled back from the impact then slumped over.

The first man reached for a holstered pistol, but Neal had sighted him in and squeezed off two more rounds. Like the other shots, these hit true too.

The man recoiled, hit the side of the house, and slid down. He was dead before his body settled onto the steps.

Neal advanced with the rifle still against his shoulder just in case anyone else came out. He stepped up to the second man and kicked his body off the steps. He leaped over the first man and entered the house. The house was dark, so it took a few seconds for his eyes to adjust, and when they did, the true carnage was evident.

The first body he came upon was an attacker.

He stepped into the living room and found Ricky and Natalie lying facedown in a pool of blood, with gunshots to their heads.

Neal had seen bodies and death, but this was different. These were people he knew and cared about. He took a deep breath and pressed forward. In the hallway he found another attacker. In the first bedroom he discovered Natalie's father; he was sprawled on the bed with several bullet holes in his chest. Neal's heart rate was off the chart and his breathing was becoming rapid. He went a few more steps down the hall but stopped short of walking into the master bedroom. He paused and took several slow and deliberate breaths. The last thing he wanted was to hyperventilate. "You got this," he reassured himself. Feeling better, he took the last remaining steps and turned into the master bedroom.

Carlos was sitting up in the bed. Two holes in his chest and one in his forehead told the story of his fate.

Neal's guts tightened. Nausea raced from the pit of his stomach and into his throat. He blinked and rubbed the stinging sweat from his eyes.

A note was stuck to Carlos' chest.

Neal walked over to his dead friend and removed the paper. He unfolded it to discover the registration for the Lincoln. In red ink Carlos' address was circled.

They had discovered the car and added two and two together. It was easy for them; Carlos didn't think to remove any trace of the car's owner. Somehow in his hubris he had missed that little detail. It was a fatal mistake, and Carlos would never get a do-over.

Neal touched his friend's hand and said, "Oh, Carlos, I'm so sorry. I'll miss you, my friend."

## CHAPTER EIGHT

*"Learn from yesterday, live for today, hope for tomorrow. The important thing is not to stop questioning."* – Albert Einstein

### Guatay, CA

Charlotte rolled over and covered her ears with the down pillow to block out Drew's snoring. To her utter disgust, Drew had decided to sleep in the same room. He was honest with her and said it was for their safety. It was the first time she believed his intention. She knew the other men were savages and couldn't be trusted, especially after what Drew had done to one of them.

The early morning light crept into the room, and for Charlotte came the promise of gathering more information to aide in her and Hope's escape. Unable to tolerate Drew's snoring, she snuck out. The musty hallway of the barn was wide, with five other doors that led to similar rooms. Were there others being held? She hadn't heard anyone, but who knew. She stealthily slipped out the back door. The outdoor air was unexpectedly crisp and cool. The back of the barn faced a tall eight-foot retaining wall with the hillside sloping away from it and out of sight. What was on the other side? Trash cans, tools, wheelbarrows and just junk sat alongside the back. A small plastic armless chair was next to the door, surrounded by dozens of cigarette butts.

She walked to one corner and looked to her right. There, a small alley separated the main barn and one of the side buildings. Behind the other building she saw similar stuff. Beyond that the ground sloped towards the chain-link fence.

A man armed with a rifle walked parallel to the fence line.

She hadn't seen anyone the day before guarding the fence, but it made perfect sense.

She turned around and looked back. The retaining wall stretched just a few feet past the smaller building on the other side of the main barn then turned left at a forty-five-degree angle. The slope of the hill above her was steep and heavily treed. Going that way to escape seemed difficult at best and impossible at worst. Being twelve, she might make it, but for Hope it would be too much.

Going anywhere near the main gate seemed foolish, as it also took them past the main house and garage, where she noticed most of the men gathered. She faced back down the hill towards the chain-link fence and said, "That looks like it's the way. Now how can I know for sure?"

"You smoke?" a raspy voice asked.

She jumped and twisted around, fear racing up

her spine. Just a few feet from her was an older man; she hadn't seen him before. He stood with his arm outstretched towards her with a pack of cigarettes.

"You smoke?" he asked again.

"No."

"You kids don't really smoke, do you? All that antismoking stuff," he quipped as he lit the cigarette.

She watched him take a long drag and exhale.

"I bet if I offered you pot, you'd smoke that?" he jested.

"I don't smoke anything."

"I thought most of you kids were dopers. You won't smoke a simple Camel Light, but you'll light up a big doobie and get stoned out of your minds."

"I don't do drugs," Charlotte declared.

"Ha." He chuckled. "So tell me, what's your story? I saw you in the yard yesterday. I'm assuming you're one of those girls who were captured."

"Who are you?" Charlotte asked. She refused to give up information freely.

"Bob."

Charlotte checked him out carefully from his tired boots where the leather had worn off the toe, exposing the steel underneath, to his tattered and stained jeans and finally his thinning V-neck T-shirt. On his head he wore a trucker's hat with the bill curled perfectly. He didn't fit the look of the others; he was more country compared to the Latin city bad-boy look the others had.

"Damn, it's chilly out here," Bob complained, rubbing his exposed arms.

"You look different than the others," she said, telling him exactly what she was thinking.

"Those guys, oh hell, I'm not one of those guys. I just work for 'em," Bob said. He attempted to blow a ring but failed.

"What do you do for them?"

"Cook."

"You're a cook?"

"I wouldn't say *I'm a cook*, like it was my career. Good God, before all this shit, I owned retail centers all over."

"So why do you cook for them now?"

"Ha, you ask a lot of questions, don't you?" Bob laughed.

"I'm curious. What else do I have to do?"

Bob shrugged and said, "I guess that's true. It's just that I've never seen a youngster like you, so full of conversation. All the kids I knew before had their heads in their phones, but someone must have taught you the lost art of talking. Anyway, what's your story? Why are you here?"

"I don't want to talk about it," Charlotte said.

"Then I guess that ends our conversation," Bob said, crushing his cigarette against the side of the building. He flicked it over the wall, turned and entered the smaller building.

Bob made sixteen, she thought. Curiosity got the best of her; she wanted to know where Bob went, so she opened the same door and poked her head inside the smaller building. A dank odor struck her first. Unable to quell the desire to know what was in there, she stepped into the dimly lit space. In the center of the room was a large table. On it she found two backpacks with the contents emptied out. She leaned over and began to examine what was there. Clothes, shoes, rope, first aid kit, lighter, compass, water bottle and a folding knife. She picked up the knife and opened it up. The stainless steel blade glinted slightly when the light from a far window hit it just right. A knife could come in handy, she thought; then in the corner of her eye she saw a wallet.

The first thing she saw was a driver's license for Timothy Brandt. He was twenty-five and from La Mesa, CA. She put it down when she saw another wallet. She picked it up too, opened it and found it belonged to Daniel Brandt; he was twenty-eight. Brothers, no doubt, she thought. An uneasy feeling came over her; she put the wallet down and stepped away from the table. All the items belonged to those two men, and more than likely they were being held captive or were dead, and if it was the former, it was at the hands of Tony and his men.

A rumbling sound startled her. She turned to see

where the sound was coming from. Slowly she walked to the far corner and saw three large refrigerators and two chest freezers. She raised her eyebrows, astonished they were working. She opened the door of the refrigerator closest to her.

Cool air washed over her first; then the light from inside lit the room around her. Inside, perishable foods were stacked on the lower shelves. Tupperware containers filled with prepared food sat on the upper shelves, with labels marking days of the week.

Out of nowhere someone grabbed her from behind. She flinched and turned to see Drew.

"What are you doing in here?" he asked.

"I couldn't sleep anymore," she replied, stepping away from him only to bump into the table.

"Not a good idea for you to be snooping around," Drew advised.

"Are we free, or are we still prisoners?" she asked.

"You're free, but not so free you can go wherever you want," Drew said, taking her arm.

She shrugged off his grip and said, "I'll go back, but never touch me again."

He snatched her arm but this time harder. "Listen here, I don't know what I have to say or do, but I'm a friend. I saved your miserable life from God knows what living hell you and your precious sister would have gone through. How about some appreciation?"

Charlotte fought back the urge to strike him. To her he represented all the men who had killed her father and taken her away from her home. However, a thought came to her. If she and Hope had any chance of surviving, she would have to play nice. She lowered her head and sighed loudly. "Sorry, I'm...I'm just so sad."

"Hey, I get it, but time heals all wounds. I know what happened to your dad was hard to see, and it couldn't have been easy to find out the truth, but if you and Hope wish to make it out of here, you're gonna have to listen to me."

"I will."

"Good. Now go back to your room. It's not safe for you to be snooping around; some of the guys are not as nice as me."

"Okay, but tell me how you have power?"

"Not for you to worry about."

"And these backpacks, they belong to two brothers, I've seen them. Are they prisoners too?" she asked, darting over to the table and pointing to the objects that lay there.

Drew advanced aggressively and ordered, "Stop asking questions and get back to the room, now."

His forceful approach gave her pause. Fearful, she stepped back, but the table prevented her from going any further.

He pointed to the back door and said, "Out."

"Fine, you don't have to yell." She stepped away from the table but not before she secretly scooped up the knife and slid it into her back pocket.

Charlotte exited with Drew right behind her.

Out of the shadows, Bob emerged. A huge grin graced his face as he said, "Aren't you a feisty one. You'll do, you'll do nicely."

## El Centro, CA

Each time Neal drove the shovel into the ground, he came away with little to show for his effort. The arid climate of the desert had sucked every last drop of moisture out of the yard, and the intensely hot desert sun baked it until it was hard.

He had been toiling away in Carlos' backyard for three hours and hadn't been able to dig more than a two-foot-deep by six-foot-long hole. At this rate he'd be digging for days. His hands ached and his back was screaming in pain, but the worst part was the diarrhea and vomiting he had been experiencing since the early morning hours.

He wasn't alone in being sick. Karen and Beth were also ill, but they were faring worse. Both of them had his symptoms but were also complaining of blurred vision, abdominal pain, and poor Beth was having a difficult time speaking coherently.

Neal was concerned and tried to provide them with comfort, but burying his friends was something that had to be done.

A strong feeling of nausea swept over him. He dropped the shovel and bent over next to the hole and heaved. Nothing came out but mucus and bile. He had emptied the contents of his stomach many hours ago and had been unable to eat since. Wiping his mouth, he continued with the task of digging the graves.

With each swing of the shovel, he began to convince himself that burying them in a shallow grave would work for now until he was feeling better.

After several more hours and three more interludes of vomiting, he was finished. He dropped the shovel and sauntered through the house. He stepped over to one of the attackers and wondered if more would come. He had to think that was possible; why wouldn't they? He thought of what he should do with their bodies and decided to let them lie where they died, at least until he was capable of disposing of them.

He slowly walked to his house. His mind spun with what they might have. Was this a flu? Was it some sort of biological weapon? Was this the second shoe that was dropping? They had survived the grid collapse only to be killed by some manmade bioweapon. It wasn't that farfetched considering the world they were living in.

He entered the house, and instantly he could smell sickness. It was thick, and it permeated everything and gave the house a somber feel.

In the back room he heard Karen coughing, or was she vomiting again? It was hard for him to tell.

A cold sweat clung to his brow. He felt horrible.

When he reached the hallway, vertigo hit him hard. His vision blurred and he lost his balance. As he fell to his knees, he unsuccessfully grabbed for anything to keep him upright. His body slammed into the floor hard, with the side of his face smashing into the floorboard.

"Karen," he mumbled.

She didn't respond.

All he could hear was her coughing loudly.

He tried to crawl but found each inch to be excruciatingly difficult. Tired, sick, dizzy and on the verge of blacking out, he used what energy he had remaining to roll onto his side and rest. The last thing he remembered was taking a deep breath and closing his eyes.

"Dada," Beth cried.

Neal opened his eyes. It was dark. He must have been asleep for hours.

"Dada," Beth again whimpered.

"I'm coming, Bethie. Dada's coming," Neal called back. He struggled but eventually got to his knees. The nausea was still there, but now he had a piercing headache and a jabbing pain in his lower guts.

"Dada," Beth moaned.

"I'm coming," he said. He got to his feet and slowly moved down the hall until he reached Beth's bedroom.

"Dada."

"I'm here, Dada's here," Neal said, rushing towards the bed but tripping before he got there. He fell into the footboard and landed on his side. "Ouch, argh."

"Dada."

"Dada's here, baby," Neal replied, finally making it to her side.

"My legs, I can't really move them," she whimpered.

Neal couldn't see well, so he found the flashlight he kept on her nightstand and clicked it on. He was shocked when he saw her.

Beth's face was already visibly gaunt. He pulled back the sheet covering her and discovered dark stains from seeping diarrhea beneath her.

His heart ached seeing her like this. Ignoring his own plight, he began rubbing her legs, hoping all they needed was circulation.

"Why are we sick?" Beth asked, her voice faint.

"It must be the flu. Let me get some medicine, okay? Um, have you been drinking any water?"

She shook her head.

"You have to drink. You have to stay hydrated," he said, knowing that he too needed to heed his advice.

"I'll be right back." He quickly stood and realized that was a mistake as the feeling of vertigo struck him again. He weaved and sat back down quickly.

Beth reached for him and tugged his arm.

"I'm going, honey," he said.

"Where's Momma?"

He took her hand and answered, "Mommy's sick too. She's in her room."

"I want Momma," Beth cried.

"Let me go get you some water and medicine. I'll also find some crackers for you to eat," Neal said as he slowly stood. Finding his legs, he exited the room and made his way to the kitchen. There he found an LED lantern and turned it on. He found the crackers, water and the children's Advil, thinking it would help.

Walking back to Beth, he stopped by his bedroom and looked in.

Karen was asleep. On the floor beside the bed

was a large bowl, most likely for vomiting into.

With her fast asleep, he made his way back to Beth.

"Here, you need to eat a few crackers," he said, offering her a single saltine.

Beth took the cracker and nibbled. "Ouch," she groaned.

"What is it?"

"My stomach, it hurts so bad."

"Here, let's get some water into you," he said, placing the bottle of water to her parched lips.

She sipped a little then gave up.

"More, you need to drink more," he insisted.

Doing as he instructed, she took a few more sips.

"I brought some medicine."

"Neal!" Karen hollered from the other room.

"You're awake. How are you feeling?" Neal yelled back.

"Come here," she pleaded.

Neal handed Beth the water and headed to Karen.

The back and forth was beginning to wear on him. His legs were weak and his entire body ached.

He sat next to her and asked, "How are you feeling?"

"Felicia, you have to go check on Felicia," Karen said.

"Okay, I will, tomorrow."

"Lucky you," Karen said.

This comment surprised him. "Lucky me? Why am I lucky?"

"You're not going to get sick," she said.

"Too late for that," he informed her.

"How? I don't understand. It's impossible," Karen said, her head shaking in doubt.

He placed his palm on her forehead. Her head felt cool, which shocked him because she should have a fever. He then recalled Beth wasn't hot either. "I'm sick, very sick."

"But you didn't eat any. It doesn't make any sense. I've been lying here, I've been racking my brain thinking what could make me and Beth so sick, and the only thing I can think that makes sense is—"

"The peaches," he said, interrupting her. It did make sense. This wasn't the flu, this was some form of food poisoning.

"But you didn't eat any," Karen said.

"You're right that I didn't eat any, but I did drink the juice from Beth's bowl," Neal informed her.

"How bad are you?" Karen asked.

Already he could tell her tone had dropped. The brief spike in energy she had was fast depleting.

"Sick, but not nearly as bad as you. Poor Bethie is real bad. She says she can't feel her legs."

"I have to see my baby," Karen said and pushed away her sheets.

"No, no, you need to rest. You also need to eat and drink water; it's critically important."

"We'll be fine. It's just food poisoning. It will be gone in a day, no more," Karen said, dismissing their illness.

"Regardless, you need to rest," Neal said, pushing her back down and covering her with the sheet. "I'll be right back. I want to go check on Beth and get her cleaned up." Neal got up slowly and left Karen.

His mind was spinning. He knew food poisoning was mostly an annoyance in the modern age, but those days were gone. A fear that plagued him often was contracting an illness, one that was common and easily eradicated before but now would prove fatal. He needed to address their symptoms, including his own, and find out what sort of food poisoning would partially paralyze Beth's legs.

## CHAPTER NINE

*"Hope is the last thing a person does before they are defeated." – Henry Rollins*

### Guatay, CA

Charlotte rose out of necessity and again left the sanctuary of her room. Listening to Drew's snoring was unbearable, and even though she had promised to stay put, she felt better knowing she had a knife for protection.

Again she was greeted with the dry, cool, crisp air. She sat down, resting her back against the cool wall, and took a deep breath. "Ahh."

This morning she had brought a friend, her diary.

Drew never returned it, and now she was happy to have it. She had found solace in the pages before, and now she hoped it would do the same.

She flipped to her last entry and began to read.

Those words jarred her emotionally as it took her back to that morning, that day she had lost her father and what was left of her innocence. A few tears gathered in the corner of her eyes, but she quickly wiped them away.

She turned to the next empty page and started to write.

"Whatcha doing?" Bob asked, seeming to appear from nowhere.

Charlotte looked up, startled; she hadn't heard him step out. "You're so sneaky."

"Good morning to you too."

"I have a question for you," Charlotte said.

"Now that doesn't surprise me," Bob quipped as he lit a cigarette.

"Do you live in there?" she asked, pointing towards the smaller building.

"Yeah."

"But you work over at the house, cooking?"

"Look at the big brain on Brad," he joked.

"Huh?"

"Oops, that was an old culture reference from a movie before your time," Bob said.

"So why a cook?" Charlotte asked. She was interested in how he came to be there.

Bob walked over and sat down opposite her, his back against the retaining wall. "It was either cook for them or die."

"They gave you an ultimatum?"

"I gave myself an ultimatum. Once the EMP hit, my business and my other skill sets became obsolete. There's no need for retail centers now."

"Wait—"

"So you see, I'm here because I told them I was a chef and had gone to culinary school, blah, blah,

blah. Anyway, the boss loves his food, and I cook him a delicious meal three times per day and make sure he has snacks too. I also cook up the family-style stuff for the other guys."

"Hold on—"

"Now, what's your story? I've told you mine."

"Just one minute, you said something about an EP," Charlotte said, frustrated that he kept cutting her off.

"The EMP? That's what turned everything off."

"What is it?"

"Something to do with a nuke or something, I guess. I don't know all the specifics, but it's the reason nothing works."

"Who did it?"

"Now that's where stuff gets tricky. There are rumors everywhere. Some say it was the Russians, others say it was the Chinese, and some even say our government did it."

"Why, why would someone do that?" Charlotte asked.

"Why? Why does anyone do what they do? Why does a bank robber rob a bank? Or why does someone rape someone? Everyone has their reasons and motives, but whoever did it wanted to get something out of it and were willing to go far to get it. It's hard to say, but does it really matter now? It's a done deal. We live in their world now and have to play by the rules that have been set for us," Bob said. His brow lowered and his jaw clenched, gone was the carefree tone he normally displayed.

"It's crazy."

"It sure is."

"If this EMP stopped everything from working, how are those refrigerators working in there?" she asked.

"Generators, solar ones, we have the panels on the roof."

"Why don't we have power in here?"

"Why waste the juice on keeping the cells lit?" Bob replied with a rhetorical question.

"Where did you get them?"

"God, you ask endless questions, don't you?"

"I'm just curious."

"Like before, you can get anything if you know where to get it. Tony has his connections. He makes trades for stuff. He got them along with all the kitchen and storage equipment months ago."

It made sense to Charlotte. The whole world wasn't suffering, so operational electronic devices would slowly make their way back.

He stared off towards the trees above them in a daze, his mind drifting to other thoughts.

Charlotte noticed he was adrift and brought him back by answering his question. "My sister and I were kidnapped, taken from our house after Tony and his people killed my dad."

He looked at her and said, "I know."

"Then why did you ask?"

"To see what you'd say."

"What else do you think you know about me?"

"I know you're thinking about escaping."

Charlotte's face turned ashen.

"Right there, I see it, I'm right. Girl, if you're going to make it in this world, you need to have a poker face, you need to hide what you're really thinking or feeling."

Annoyed and equally scared, she jumped up. "You don't know me."

"I know you better than you think."

"What if I go tell Drew, or worse tell Tony, you lied and that you're not really a chef? Huh? What would happen to you?"

"You won't do that."

"How do you know?"

"First, you don't know if I'm full of shit, and second, I have something on you."

"Oh, that you think I'm going to try to escape? Really, that's what you're going to tell them? Of course it would only be natural to think about it."

Bob stood and tossed the butt of his cigarette; he stepped up to her and leaned close to her face.

Not wanting him to think she was frightened, she stood her ground and didn't flinch.

"You won't say anything because I don't think you'd want me to tell the boss you stole a knife and might be angling to use it in some grand escape plan."

Charlotte's face turned white.

He lifted his finger and pointed it in her face. "Again you show your cards. Girl, I won't hurt you."

"Please don't tell them."

"I won't."

"Thank you."

Bob stepped away, but before going back inside, he turned and said, "Do you want to know why I won't tell them?"

"Why?"

"It's not because you have something on me, nope, it's not that. It's because you and me have the same objective."

"We do?"

"I want to get the hell out of here just as bad as you do."

## El Centro, CA

Neal woke suddenly. Was it something he heard? Did he sense someone? He looked right and out towards the living room from the big chair he had positioned himself in during the night in an attempt to stand watch.

He looked on the floor and saw his rifle at his feet. Maybe it was a noise; maybe it was his rifle falling to the floor.

The midday sun beamed in and hurt his eyes. He squinted, raised his hand to shade his face, and tried to stand, but found it almost impossible. His legs felt heavy. Using his arms, he rubbed them. "What the hell?" he grumbled.

The house was eerily quiet.

"Karen," he called out.

Nothing.

"Bethie, you up?"

Still nothing.

His legs felt odd, like they were asleep but without the pins and needles. He looked around for something to grab hold of but saw nothing within reach. Looking down, he saw his rifle. An idea came, so he grabbed it and, with its muzzle down, used it like a crutch to lift himself out of the chair. He grunted until he stood tall.

"Karen, you awake?" he hollered.

An unintelligible mumble came from the master bedroom. This was a sign both good and bad. She was still alive, but she was still sick.

He hobbled to the bedroom and found her lying almost like he had left her the night before. "How ya doing?" he asked.

She slowly raised her hand.

"I'm going to check on Bethie," he informed her and moved towards her room. There he saw his beautiful daughter lying still. A sudden fear struck him. He moved quickly from the doorway to her bedside in seconds. He rolled her over and checked her pulse. Finding a slight pulse, he breathed a sigh of relief; however, she didn't look good. "Sweetheart, wake up. I need you to wake up and drink some water."

Beth opened her eyes slightly and whispered, "Dada."

"Baby girl, I need you to drink some water."

His concern heightened when he saw her pillow cover had bloodstains on it. He lifted her weak and limp body with one arm and with the other grabbed the water bottle off her nightstand and put it to her lips. "Drink, baby, please."

Beth opened her mouth a crack and sipped.

"More, you need to drink more."

She began to cough. Her cough then turned into heaving. With each heave her little body shook. Blood mixed with mucus and bile drooled from her open mouth. Tears followed as she looked at him and said, "I feel like I can't breathe."

"Honey, I know it's difficult, but you need to drink something," he said. He had to get fluids in her or she would die from that.

An idea popped in his head. He remembered

Carlos had a box of IV fluid in his garage. If he could get an IV into her, she'd be fine. He laid her back down and rushed as fast as his battered body would take him. He too was in need of fluids and nourishment. It had been days since he had eaten, and his body was suffering for it. He reached the front door, swung it open, and the last people he needed to see were standing in the cul-de-sac. He froze. Unsure if they had seen him, he stepped back into the shadows of his house. By a rough count he saw six heavily armed men. They were searching the bodies of their fallen comrades and inspecting the vehicles.

The men talked back and forth, but it was hard for Neal to understand fully, as he could only hear a word here or there.

They pointed towards Carlos' house and swarmed it with their rifles at the ready.

Neal went to the spare room to get his rifle, but it wasn't there. He then remembered using it as a crutch, and he had left it in Beth's room. Not hesitating, he went there and found it leaning against her chest of drawers. He snatched it and headed back to the spare room. There he'd get a better view of the men.

The men cleared Carlos' house and reassembled outside.

Neal was in his chair and watching intently. The

excitement caused by their presence temporarily made him forget he was sick.

They huddled and were chatting.

Again, it was impossible for him to hear what they were saying.

One man tore away from the group and headed towards Neal's house.

Neal shouldered his rifle and leveled the sights on the man.

Several of the men hollered and waved for the one man to return.

The one man stopped and came back to the circle and began to wave his arms as if he was arguing.

"Dada," Beth cried.

Neal's heart just about jumped out of his chest. He resisted leaving the window, but he needed to see what Beth wanted. He raced through the house, hoping to stop her from calling out again. He arrived at her door to find her on the floor. He rushed to her and asked, "You okay?"

"I had to go potty. I didn't want to…" she said, embarrassed by the fact she had messed her pajamas.

"It's fine, honey, it is," he said, lifting her up. For his weakened state she felt like she weighed two hundred pounds. He got her back in bed and covered her. "I'll be right back to clean you up," he said and headed back to his spot in the spare room. He was panicked now. Would they be there still? Were they headed towards his house and about to enter? He ran all the worst-case scenarios through his mind in the mere seconds it took him to get back in place. When he looked out the window and saw them, they weren't coming his way, but they were interfering with saving Beth's life because they were emptying out Carlos' garage.

They rummaged and tore through the boxes of supplies Carlos had stockpiled.

"Please, oh God, please don't touch the IVs," he said out loud.

Neal watched for fifteen precious minutes as they ripped through the garage and took what they thought valuable.

When they were finished, they again gathered and chatted.

Neal feared they would come to his house, looking for more.

A radio crackled to life on one man's hip. He pulled it off and replied. A back and forth conversation occurred.

"Please leave, go, fucking go," Neal said.

And just like that, the man with the radio ordered all the others into the vehicles, including the Suburban Carlos had stolen and the Lincoln, and drove away.

Neal gulped loudly as he watched them make the

# HOPE

turn off the street and disappear. With them gone, he went to go see if the IVs were taken.

The garage was a total mess, boxes turned over and their contents emptied. Personal belongings and items valuable only to Carlos and his family were trampled on.

In that instant Neal paused and looked at a family photo album on the garage floor. Photos of Carlos and Natalie as kids were loose and spread all over. A painful tug at his heart made him miss his life before. He knelt down and picked up one of the photos; it was of Carlos and Natalie on one of their first dates. Seeing the smiling faces in the photo, it made him feel sorry that these men cared so little for another's life. Gone was sincerity and caring; it was lost to this new brutal world. Those men cared nothing for anyone but their own basic need. None stopped to appreciate that the belongings they were trashing had actually been someone's and they had taken care of and put value on them. The world was insane, the inhumanity of mankind was thriving, and there wasn't a thing he could do about it.

In his peripheral vision he caught sight of a small first aid kit. This snapped him back to the task at hand of finding the IVs. He pocketed the photo and started looking. From one box to the next then on to the cabinets, he looked. Nothing. He went into the house and tore through every spot, but came up empty-handed.

The frustration was killing him, but it was also keeping him moving, as a heavy fatigue weighed on him.

After spending an hour, he gave up; it wasn't there. Either Carlos never had them, or those men had taken them. He'd never know.

Exhausted and angry, he lamented the fact of going back home empty-handed, but he needed to try to get Beth to drink and hopefully eat.

Back in his house, he went directly to Beth's room and found her asleep. He couldn't have her sleeping in soiled clothes, so he removed them and with a box of baby wipes cleaned her up.

As he wiped her down, he couldn't help but notice how thin she looked. It had been days and she already was looking poorly.

What kind of food poisoning could take this long to get over? he asked himself. Needing to know, he headed to his office and found a medical journal. He flipped to the back and looked up food poisoning, found the starting page, and went to it. He quickly scanned the symptoms of *Salmonella* and *E. coli*, but their symptoms didn't match exactly. He then saw botulism and read that it could cause paralysis, slurred speech, muscle weakness, eyelid drooping and difficulty swallowing, which sounded almost to a tee what they all had to some varying degree. He skimmed over the rest and went directly to treatments. As he read each word, the tension increased. There wasn't a home remedy for botulism. They all needed emergency medical care, according to the book, and like he suspected, the fluids were critical, and the way they recommended delivery was via IV. His heart sank.

He plopped into his office chair and thought about what he should do and came to the conclusion there wasn't much. He needed those IVs, but that wasn't an option right now. Not satisfied, he opened the book again and continued reading. He had to find a way because if he failed, his failure would mean certain death for his family.

Guatay, CA

Drew stepped into the room with a broad smile and said, "It's dinnertime." In his right hand he balanced three trays, and in his left he had two sodas. "I've got a surprise for you," he said, holding up the sodas.

"We don't drink soda," Charlotte said.

"It's root beer," Drew said happily.

"Can we have root beer floats?" Hope asked.

"I wish we could, but that's not going to happen," Drew answered.

Charlotte went back to writing in her diary.

Drew slid her tray over next to her and said,

"There's also another surprise."

Not interested in his games, she kept writing but still asked, "What?"

"Look," Drew insisted.

Irritated, she looked over and saw a package of Twinkies on her tray. "We don't eat Twinkies either."

"Who doesn't eat Twinkies?" Drew asked rhetorically.

"We don't."

Hope then defied her sister and said, "I do, yep."

"No, you don't," Charlotte challenged.

"Yes, I do. One time Mommy let me have one."

"Not true," Charlotte barked.

"Is true. You weren't there, I was," Hope declared.

"Figures, you were the spoiled baby in the family," Charlotte shot back.

Hope ignored Charlotte and went for the Twinkie first.

"You should know the Twinkie was a gift from Chef Bob."

Hearing Bob's name caught Charlotte's attention. "What did he say?"

Seeing how urgent she was with her question, Drew decided to play a game with her. "You should have heard what he said, wow, that's the only word I have for it."

"What?"

"He said...tell the girls I gave them a treat," Drew said.

"And?"

"That was it. Why are you being so dramatic? Plus, what do you care what Bob says?" Drew asked.

"I don't. I just talked with him the other day is all."

"Don't mess around with any of the guys. You can't trust a single one," Drew informed her as he stuffed a fork full of beans into his mouth.

"But we can trust you?" Charlotte quipped.

"You are tough. Good God, yes, you can trust me. I did save your damn lives," Drew snapped. He got up and sat next to Hope. "Say, you want to play Go Fish."

"Sure," Hope happily replied.

"Was your sister always grumpy?" Drew asked Hope.

Hope didn't answer; she looked at Charlotte and softly said, "No, she used to be nicer."

Like a petulant child, Charlotte stuck her tongue out at Hope. She put her head down and continued writing in her diary. She knew she had to be more easygoing but found it difficult, almost impossible.

Drew and Hope laughed as they played cards.

Their laughter irritated Charlotte even more. She paused from her writing and looked at them. She felt like Hope was betraying her parents' memory, specifically her father's, by playing nice and having fun. How dare she have fun? She sighed heavily as she stared at a new blank page. What would she write? The messages to her mother now seemed silly. Her mother would never find them, and that was considering she was even alive. She wanted to believe her mother was still out there, but with each day that passed, she lost a little more hope that she'd ever see her again.

She chewed on her lip. What could she write? The blank page stared back at her, taunting her to write something. Charlotte pressed her eyes closed and cleared her thoughts. She wanted to give in and see what would come to her organically.

A thought jumped into her head. Like a light bulb turning on and vanquishing the darkness, she knew what she needed to write. Excited, she put the pen to page and began to write feverishly.

## CHAPTER TEN

"There was never a night or a problem that could defeat sunrise or hope." – Bernard Williams

### El Centro, CA

Neal couldn't remember dozing off, but obviously he had. He jerked up and again felt the vertigo that had been plaguing him. His legs felt heavy as he tried to stand. His vision was blurry, so he blinked heavily several times to clear it, but it only worked a little.

The medical journal fell from his lap onto the floor with a thud.

He looked at it and now remembered he was up researching what he could do to save Beth and Karen, and he must have just passed out from exhaustion.

Within arm's reach was his rifle. Like before he used it as a crutch and lifted up. When he was steady and confident, he took a few steps and paused.

Once more the house was eerily quiet.

By the way the light cast through the window, he could tell it was late morning.

He got to his bedroom and saw Karen.

She was on the far side of the bed now and not moving.

He took a labored step in the room and was

greeted by a strong stench. His poor bride was lying in soiled sheets and clothes. He had given so much attention to Beth, and in his own weakened state, he hadn't been taking as good care of her as he wanted.

When he arrived at the bedside, he rejoiced in getting to sit down.

His movements woke her. She motioned with her hand and said above a whisper, "Neal, is that you?"

"Yeah."

"How's Bethie?"

"Not sure, I'm checking on her next."

It took all the energy she had to shift from her side to her back. When she saw him, she cracked a smile. "Hi, love."

He extended his arm and took her hand. "I love you, babe. I promise I'll get you cleaned up."

"Oh, you don't like my new smell, eau du sickness?" she joked.

He chuckled. Oh, how he loved her. Even in the depth of her illness she was able to find humor.

"Please go check on Beth," she said.

"How are you?"

"To be honest, I feel like shit. I'm so weak, and the cramps are excruciating, and my throat feels like it's squeezing."

"I need you to drink water and eat. You have to eat too."

"I will. Now go check on Bethie."

He stood and turned but stopped when she called out.

"I know this is stupid, but did you ever check on Felicia?"

He shook his head.

"I know you're sick too, but if you feel better, please go. She must be suffering."

"Botulism, that's what this is, I think."

"Botulism? How long will we be sick for, do you know?"

He didn't have the heart to tell her the prognosis was fifty-fifty if left untreated with the proper antitoxins and without adequate hydration, so he lied, "Soon, but you have to drink water," he said then left. He paused just outside of Beth's room and took a deep breath. He couldn't quite fill his lungs; it was the oddest feeling.

Looking through the beams of light that cut through Beth's room, he could see her small body lying still. "Beth, sweetheart, it's Dada. Good morning," he whispered as he walked in. He came to the side of her bed and was happy to sit down.

She didn't move when he sat.

He touched her arm and instantly recoiled. Something was wrong. Her arm felt stiff and cold.

"Beth?" he said, turning and pulling her towards him.

Her body rolled to reveal the depressing fact that she was dead.

"Beth! Beth!" he exclaimed as he frantically ran his hands all over her body, touching her throat to check for a pulse, opening her mouth, and touching her chest. He rested his ear and listened for a heartbeat, but nothing. Her body was cold and stiff. "No, no, please God, no!" Neal gripped his daughter's small body tight to him as he began to sob uncontrollably; his greatest fear was in the room with him. Like a thief in the night, death was in his house. Worse yet it was the one death he couldn't bear. He was brought back by Karen's shouts.

"Neal, what's going on?" Karen yelled. By his tone she knew something was wrong.

"Karen, don't come in here, don't you dare," Neal insisted. Resigned to the fact she was gone, he scooped up her small body and held her close to him. Tears exploded from his eyes and poured down his heavily stubbled face.

A loud crash came from the master bedroom. "Beth, it's Mommy. Talk to me," Karen hollered, her voice cracking with fear.

"Karen, she's gone. Our baby is gone," Neal moaned.

Karen's legs were too weak to carry her, so she crawled. "Bethie, talk to Mommy."

Neal wailed.

Dragging her worthless legs, Karen dragged herself to Beth's bedside and grabbed onto Neal's leg.

With his left arm, Neal pulled her up and onto the bed.

Together they embraced Beth's body.

There was nothing they could do. Fate had taken their daughter.

Never in his life had Neal felt so powerless. His duty as a parent was to protect his child, and he had failed. He would never forgive himself or ever seek to be forgiven; he had failed and would always hold himself responsible.

Guatay, CA

Charlotte and Hope were sitting in the back alley of the barn. Charlotte with her diary and Hope with her teddy bear, Cuddles.

Drew came out the back door and smiled when he saw them. "Hi, girls."

"Hi, Drew," Hope replied.

"Hi," Charlotte said.

"Wow, I got a *hi*. Things are looking up." Drew laughed.

"Do you want to play Go Fish?" Hope asked.

"Not now, but later. I've got some good news," Drew said.

"Yeah," Hope said.

"You are the eternal optimist," Drew said to Hope, rubbing her shoulder.

"Do you have to begin each piece of news with *I got news?* How about just telling us?" Charlotte snarled.

"There's the girl I know, and I thought the greeting meant we were getting somewhere," Drew quipped.

"Tell us, tell us," Hope said.

"We're going somewhere, together," Drew said.

"Yippie, I hope it's somewhere fun," Hope said, hopping up and down.

"God, you're such a loser," Charlotte barked at Hope.

"Shut up, you're mean," Hope shot back.

"You're an idiot. Don't you care that these people killed Dad? You act like they're your friends; they're not," Charlotte barked.

"Calm down," Drew ordered.

"I want to go home; then I'll calm down, okay?" Charlotte said, slamming her diary closed and jumping to her feet.

"I've told you before, give it time. If you keep acting like a damn brat, you won't get past the gates ever," Drew yelled.

Hope stood with her hands over her ears.

"Charlotte, I would leave you here alone while I

go with Hope, but I can't. I won't, it's too risky. So get your stuff; we're leaving in ten minutes."

"Where?" Charlotte asked.

"It's a surprise," Drew said.

"I'll look after her," Bob said. He was standing in the doorway of the side building, smoking a cigarette.

"No, thanks," Drew said.

"Yeah, I'll stay here. Bob will look after me."

Drew leaned in close to Charlotte and said, "He's a dirty old man. Don't trust that crusty old man."

"But I should trust you?" Charlotte asked mockingly.

"Yeah, you can."

"I'm staying here, and you can't make me go," Charlotte said defiantly.

The veins in Drew's neck were pulsating with anger; he glared at Charlotte then turned his gaze on Bob. "If you're going to stay here, take this," Drew said, handing her a four-inch-blade knife.

With wide-eyed enthusiasm, Charlotte took the knife and pulled it out of its leather sheath.

"If anyone tries anything, stick them."

"Can I have a gun?" Charlotte asked, hoping she could up the bargain.

"Hell no, at least not yet."

"Why?" she asked.

"Because I don't trust you, that's why."

"So you think I'll shoot you?" Charlotte asked.

Drew cocked his head and replied, "Yeah, I do."

"You're right, I probably would," Charlotte snarled.

Bob burst out with laughter.

Drew again glared Bob's way.

Bob leaned back and took a long drag of his cigarette.

"We'll be back in a couple hours," Drew said as he directed Hope back inside.

The door closed with a clack.

Charlotte looked at Bob, raised the knife and said, "Look at that."

"You're a keen one. I'll be keeping my eye on you, that's for sure," Bob joked, insinuating she might be a threat to him. He tossed the butt of his cigarette and opened the door to leave.

"Hold on, wait. Let's talk," Charlotte pleaded.

"Then come on," he said, waving for her to follow him inside.

She took a step but hesitated.

"It's fine. Plus you've got that knife; I won't mess with ya."

From an early age her father advised her to trust her gut instincts and intuition, but she pushed those aside and followed him.

He pointed to the table she'd seen before and

said, "Grab a seat. I'll be right back."

She walked to the table and sat. The items she'd seen before were gone. The table was clear except for a couple half-empty water bottles.

Bob returned and tossed a bag of M&Ms on the table.

She jumped when the hard candies hit the thick wood tabletop.

"There's more where that came from," he said and took a seat across from her.

"I don't eat candy," she said again, reprising the healthy-eating shtick she had told Drew.

"What kid doesn't eat candy?"

"Me."

"What are you fucking worried about? You ain't gonna get fat, not in this world. I look at it this way, best to eat what's in front of you because you never know if that will be your last meal."

"I just don't eat—"

"Oh God, don't tell me you're one of the many allergic types. What is it with your generation? All the helicopter mommies and allergic kids who sit around bitching because they never got a trophy for coming in last," Bob said, mocking her.

"I'm not allergic. We...um, I don't eat bad food."

"Is that what your mommy or daddy taught you?" Again Bob hit her with a scornful mocking tone.

"Sugar isn't good for you."

"I like to size people up, and you're one of them."

"One of what?"

"Those spoiled entitled kids who got everything and could eat all the candy they wanted, but you didn't because *'sugar is bad for you'*," he said, holding up his hand and adding quotations with his fingers.

"Why did you want to look after me then treat me so mean?" Charlotte snapped.

"What are you going to do, go cry and tell your new daddy?"

Charlotte jumped up and hustled towards the door.

"Wait, wait," Bob urged.

"No."

"C'mon, I'm just busting your…I'm just teasing."

"I don't need to sit here and listen to this."

"I'm sorry," Bob pleaded.

Charlotte ignored him and kept walking.

"I know how we can escape," Bob blurted out.

Charlotte froze. She turned and said, "How?"

"Sit down, eat your M&Ms, or don't eat them, I don't care, but I do need you to listen."

Charlotte walked back and sat down. She looked at the candy and was tempted, but after the back and forth, eating the candies would equal defeat.

"How serious are you about getting outta here?" he asked.

"Serious."

"I'm asking because if you run away and get caught, they just might kill you and your little sister."

"Can I ask you a question?"

He nodded.

"Drew bought us out of slavery. Why can't we leave?"

"Because you're not really free. He owns you; Drew owns you."

"But he said he'll let us go soon."

"He's lying. That boy has a taste for...let's just say he likes to date young girls."

Charlotte scrunched her face and said, "Yuck, that's so gross."

"Me, I like them—"

"Stop, I don't want to hear," she said, holding up her hand.

"So you're serious?" he asked.

"After what you just told me, more than I was before."

"Good."

"Why do you want to leave?" she asked, genuinely curious as to his motive.

"At first it made sense to join; it was either that or die. Now I just want the hell outta here. The boss is an unstable man, and his crew are cutthroats. You can't trust a one of them. I'd feel safer on the open road than with this group."

"Where will we go?"

"Me, I'm going to Argentina."

"Why go there?"

"I love to tango," he joked.

"Huh?"

"It's as far away from this insanity as one can get without hanging out with the penguins."

"I don't want to go to Argentina."

Bob laughed and asked, "Who said you're coming with me?"

"I thought."

"I'll get you back to your house, and from there we say our farewells. I can't have two little girls dragging me down."

Looking a bit let down, Charlotte began to fiddle with the bag of candy but stopped short of opening them.

He watched her and wanted again to tease her but kept it to himself. "There's one thing that happens here that everyone can count on. It's like fucking clockwork. Every Friday night at nine, the boss has a party, right out in the yard there."

Charlotte leaned in to listen more intently.

Bob started to chuckle. "At first I thought these guys rock, they're awesome. I still remember my first

Friday party; then shit got real." He stopped and looked down.

Charlotte waited for him to continue, but he remained quiet.

"What got real?" she asked.

"Well, you'll see. Tomorrow is Friday."

"Tell me."

"These devils bring debauchery to another level. They first start with the Friday fights. They have two people, prisoners always, fight it out to the death. It's always best for them if they're family. It's disgusting, sick. They cheer and make those poor bastards fight and kill each other with their bare hands. Then after that they bring in the women—"

"Enough."

"But Fridays are the best time to get the fuck out of Dodge. Most of the men are drunk as hell, and the others are paying too much attention to the fights to notice a lot. It's our best time to sneak out of here."

Charlotte thought about the wallets she had found. She guessed they were brothers, and now it added up. They had captured those two young men and were going to use them for entertainment.

Bob snapped his fingers. "You here?"

Charlotte was lost in thought but quickly snapped back, "How do we leave?"

"First you have to get away from your boyfriend—"

"Stop saying that."

"Fine, you have to get away from *Drew*."

"How do I do that?"

"You figure it out; just make sure you and your sister are out back here at nine."

"Then?"

"Then we go down to the fence line, the one below us. I know the guard rotation, so I know who will be there. I've been giving him homemade booze and snacks on the side for months. He won't suspect anything, as I make it a point to go down to see him on his shifts."

"No car?"

"That's too risky. We're going to have to go on foot. Getting a car is just about impossible. Tony has the vehicles locked down tight. If we make a play for one, it could blow the whole plan."

"How far do we have to walk home?" Charlotte asked.

Bob jumped up and grabbed a map from his room and quickly returned. He unfolded it and pointed to where they were. "We're here."

She leaned in and asked, "Is this it?" She pointed at a circle up in the hills with the address written in pencil.

"Yes, right there." Bob pointed, jabbing his finger at a spot on the map.

"We're not too far from my house."

"So where are you from?"

"Descanso, just a little to the west along the highway here," Charlotte said.

"Good."

"So if we head out this way, we'll have the cover of night and the Cleveland National Forest. We'll parallel Old Highway 80 here until we get to Descanso."

"Hope and I won't need your help once we get out of here. We should be fine," Charlotte said confidently once she knew exactly where they were. Charlotte then thought of Tony and the rest of the men. It was an unresolved issue, especially for her and Hope. "How do we prevent Tony and his men from coming after us?"

"Let me work on that. I've got a plan that will ensure we never hear from Tony or his men again."

Beyond curious, she asked, "What?"

"That's for me to worry about. You have your responsibilities and I have mine."

"I'll take care of Drew, don't you worry."

Bob sat back and gave her a smug look.

She too leaned back. Happy to know they weren't far from home and feeling that their ordeal would be over soon, she gave in and grabbed the peanut M&Ms. She tore the package and poured a few into her hand. "I like the green ones."

He gave her a look and said, "I thought you

didn't eat candy."

"I don't normally, but I'm a kid, it's what we do."

"So you bullshitted me?"

"Yes and no, Mom didn't like us to eat a ton of sugar, but that didn't mean we never ate it. I had you believing that. Now who's the one who was fooled?"

"Touché," Bob said. "Just make sure you and your sister are out back tomorrow at nine."

"We will be; you can count on it," she said, tossing a few candies in her mouth.

## CHAPTER ELEVEN

"Forgiving does not erase the bitter past. A healed memory is not a deleted memory. Instead, forgiving what we cannot forget creates a new way to remember. We change the memory of our past into a hope for our future." – Lewis B. Smedes

### El Centro, CA

"You made me a promise once, do you remember that?" Karen asked, her hand in Neal's.

"Yes, yes, I do," he replied.

"What was that?"

"Now is not the time."

She squeezed his hand with all her strength. "What was it?" she asked again, insisting he answer, as if saying it out loud would make it real.

Neal grimaced but honored her request. "That I'd make this world a better place."

She smiled and said, "You declared that the day Beth was born. You kept that promise, even after everything happened; you kept making our world better."

Neal began to sob.

Karen petted his head as tears streamed down both of their faces.

"Please don't leave me," he moaned.

"Make me another promise."

"I can't."

"You must."

"I can't," he cried.

She lifted his head and looked through his eyes and into his soul. "Promise me that you'll live on. Promise me you'll survive this."

"I can't make that promise."

"You must, because you're the only one left that will keep us alive. If you die, no one will say our names; you must survive and carry on."

Neal lowered his head, tears raining down.

"Promise me," she begged.

"I promise," he relented.

Squeezing his hand with what little strength she had, she said, "Thank you."

"You can't leave me, you can't."

"You're going to hate me."

"Why would you say that?"

"I need you to promise me something else."

In what could be her last moments, he was resolved to make her happy. "Anything."

"You're a strong man, a good man. I want you to survive so you can help people. Promise me you'll help those in need, those who are weak and innocent. Be their strength, be the rock they can cling to for salvation."

Neal slowly shook his head and said, "I don't

think I'm that man. I wasn't strong enough to save Beth. I wasn't smart enough to know something like this could happen to us. I didn't prepare; I wasn't ready."

"Oh, sweetheart, don't do this, don't torture yourself. You're a good man with a noble heart. I'm angry at the world, but not you, you're my soul mate, my one true love. I'm just so sad that I won't be with you."

"Karen, you can't give up. You have to fight."

"Where's Bethie? Have you buried her yet? Please tell me you haven't."

"In her bed, she's lying there like an angel. She looks like she's just sleeping."

"Take me to her; carry me to her, please."

His entire body shook, and the weakness he felt wouldn't stop him from fulfilling her wish. He stood up, shoved his arms under her frail frame, and lifted.

With her arm around his neck, she rested against his shoulder.

With every ounce of strength and determination, he walked the distance to Beth's bedroom and placed Karen next to their daughter's lifeless body.

Karen instantly curled up next to Beth's body and began to cry loudly. "My little baby, I'm so sorry, I'm so sorry."

Neal fell to his knees and sobbed more.

Karen petted Beth, running her fingers through

her hair. "My little baby, my poor baby."

Neal grabbed Beth's cold hand and kissed it. He'd give anything to have her back, but it was all too late. He was losing his family, and there wasn't anything he could do about it.

"Can you get me some water?" Karen asked.

He looked up and towards the nightstand. The glass there was empty. "I'll be right back." He braced his weight against the footboard and stood. He stumbled out of the bedroom and towards the kitchen. He tore the kitchen apart, looking for fresh drinking water, but couldn't find any. "Damn it!" he groaned. Knowing more cases of bottled water were in the garage, he headed there.

After finding the water, he made his way back. When he reached Beth's bedroom door, he looked in and saw them lying still. He took that moment to reflect, take a mental snapshot. These two were his purpose, his life. Without them, life wasn't worth living. He entered the room and said, "Sorry it took me so long."

Karen didn't respond.

He unscrewed the cap and with a shaking hand offered it to Karen.

Still she didn't move.

He looked closer and could see her eyes were open but lifeless. "Karen?"

Nothing.

He dropped the open water and crawled up on the bed. "Karen, Karen, wake up."

The weight of his body on the bed made her head roll easily.

He placed his fingers on her neck and prayed he'd find a pulse, but there was nothing.

"Karen, no, Karen, please God, no!" he cried and slumped over them. He turned his gaze towards the ceiling and screamed out, "NO!"

Guatay, CA

Hope couldn't stop talking about the day trip she and Drew had taken yesterday. On and on she kept mentioning it.

Only after Charlotte heard they had gone to her house to get toys and other things did she regret not going.

She was grateful that Drew had thought of her enough to bring fresh clothes. She just wished she could have seen the house, but it didn't matter, she'd be seeing it soon enough.

The concerns about Tony and his men following her and Hope home made her anxious. She was sure they'd go looking for them, and it was natural to think they'd go to her house. Bob himself couldn't give her assurances, so it was a big risk.

As Hope played with the toys she had brought

back, Charlotte sat in silence, her diary next to her.

"You want to play with me?" Hope asked.

"No, I'm busy," Charlotte replied.

"You don't look busy," Hope said.

"I'm thinking."

"About what?"

"I'll tell you later."

Hope jumped over to her and said, "Tell me now."

Charlotte was hard on Hope, even more so since losing their father. She deeply loved her little sister, and never had she ever felt jealousy for her. Even when Hope was born, Charlotte rejoiced in having a baby sister and made it her mandate to take care of her.

Hope wasn't a planned birth. She happened as a result of making up after a bitter argument, or that was what she heard her parents joke about. Being twice Hope's age did make the reason seem legit, but if she was an accident, her parents never showed her. Their affection for Hope was poignant and intense.

"Do you trust me?" Charlotte asked.

"Yes."

"So if I say you need to do something and it was very important, you'd do it without asking questions?"

"Yes."

"Good."

"Why?"

Charlotte smiled. If Hope could be described as one thing, it was curious. This, of course, would mean you'd have to negate her being the happiest child ever, but putting aside her happiness, Hope was constantly asking questions. She thirsted for knowledge and had an intellectual curiosity.

Without asking, Hope gave Charlotte a hug.

"What was that for?" Charlotte asked.

"You look unhappy, and remember what Mommy said…"

"Sometimes a hug is all you need to make it all feel better," Charlotte said, repeating one of their mother's common sayings.

"Do you feel better?" Hope asked.

"I do."

"Good. Now do you want to play with me?" Hope asked innocently.

Knowing she wouldn't find the answer that very second, Charlotte decided to just be and play with Hope. Like their mother also said, "Live in the now and appreciate that special moment because once it's gone, it's gone forever."

## El Centro, CA

Neal lay with his family for hours. He fell asleep several times and woke with the hope they'd be alive and that it was all some horrible nightmare; but it wasn't a nightmare, it was worse than one. His worst visions had come true. He felt as if someone had ripped his guts out and seared his heart with a hot poker. Death was something he welcomed. He wanted more than anything to have his illness take him too, but deep down he felt he was slowly recovering. Was it because he was stronger than them or that he had only ingested a little juice? Did that matter?

After all the reading, he knew that the survival rate was fifty percent if left untreated. Was it a numbers game and his family lost? For him death was welcome to come snatch him away. There was nothing to live for now. There was no purpose, no reason to take another breath.

He lay staring at the ceiling. He kept going over the reasons why they died and he didn't in a weak attempt to justify what happened, but alas, it was stupid to. His mind then shifted to satisfying his last desire. If his illness wasn't going to take him, maybe he should do it himself. It would give him back one thing he had lost: his ability to control his life.

With renewed purpose and a plan, he got up and started the preparations for his final act.

## Guatay, CA

Charlotte rarely chewed her fingernails, but now was an exception. She paced the back alley behind the barn, watching the sun slowly descend in the west.

The energy of the compound was increasing with each degree the sun lowered, in anticipation of the evening's festivities.

Drew too was especially amped. He had come to the girls' room earlier and told them he had a surprise he would share later, one that would make them happy.

Charlotte was curious as to what it was but equally skeptical.

Drew hadn't taken away the knife he had given her days before, so she proudly wore it on her hip.

Bob stepped out into the alley and lit a cigarette. He walked up to her and asked, "You'll be here at nine, right?"

"I said yes."

"Okay, because this has to happen without a glitch."

"I know."

Bob adjusted his loose-fitting jeans and with a cracked smile asked, "So whatcha gonna do about pretty boy?"

Charlotte's only reply was a movement of her right hand to the hilt of the knife on her hip.

"Ha, you're gonna stick him?"

"Maybe," she replied, acting cocky.

"Really? You're tougher than I thought. You're one ruthless little bitch." Bob cackled.

Charlotte twisted her face in anger and snapped, "You just make sure you're ready, because we will be."

"I will, my plan isn't foolproof, but if it works, we shouldn't be hearing from Tony or his guys again."

Satisfied, she turned and walked back inside. A heavy feeling hit her. Would she be able to subdue Drew? Would she be capable when it mattered most? It was easy to act tough, another to be tough.

Lost in her thoughts, she stepped in the room and found Drew kneeling in front of a half-naked Hope. Her emotions went from shock to anger. "What are you doing?"

Drew turned around, surprised by Charlotte's abrupt and angry tone. "I, ah."

"You're sick; get your hands off my sister!" Charlotte yelled.

"I, ah, I was just…" he said, attempting to defend his actions.

Charlotte's blood was boiling. She could hear Bob's voice echoing in her head to prove she was not the entitled little brat he thought she was. "Get away from her!"

Hope squirmed away and ran to the corner of the room.

"Hey, I was just helping her," Drew said, standing, his arms raised in a defensive position.

Charlotte pulled the knife from the sheath and advanced. "You're sick, I knew it."

"No, you're misunderstanding; I was just helping her—"

"You're sick, sick, sick," Charlotte screamed and lunged at him.

She landed on top of Drew. Her weight and the force she came at him with caused him to fall to the ground.

"Charlotte, stop this. You're acting crazy," Drew said.

"Bob said you liked little girls. He was right," Charlotte declared, taking the knife and swinging it down into Drew's shoulder.

Drew howled in pain.

She withdrew the knife and came down again. This time the knife struck him in his chest.

Drew gasped once then died, his eyes wide open.

Charlotte pulled the knife out and struck one more time. Her rage had blinded her to the fact he was dead.

Hope was curled up in the corner, crying.

Blood began to pool around Drew.

Charlotte took a deep breath and looked down at

what she had done. She pulled the knife from his chest, looked at the thick blood dripping off the blade, and finally realized she had done something horrible. She dropped the knife and leapt off his body. "What have I done?"

"Why, why did you kill him?" Hope sobbed.

"He was...um, he was trying to hurt you," Charlotte replied, rocking back and forth, her legs pulled up tight against her chest.

"No, he wasn't. He was helping me put on the dress he got me. He got you one too," Hope yelled.

"No, you're wrong. He was trying to hurt you," Charlotte said.

"He was helping me. He got us dresses to wear, our favorites from the house," Hope screamed, tears flowing heavily down her face.

"No, he wasn't, he was a bad person," Charlotte said. She jumped to her feet and went to Hope. "Take my hand. We have to go."

Hope looked at Charlotte's blood-covered hand and kicked at her. "No, I'm not going with you, you're crazy!"

Charlotte looked at the grisly scene and knew they had to push up their plans. "Come with me. We have to leave, now!"

"No!"

"Come now," Charlotte barked, grabbing Hope by the arm.

"Ouch, you're hurting me!" Hope yelled.

Charlotte dragged her across the room to a wall locker. She opened the doors and froze when she saw the dresses.

"Let go of me," Hope yelled.

Charlotte reached out and touched the pink pastel dress her parents had bought her just before all the troubles occurred. She touched the silky sleeve then recoiled when the blood from her hand stained it. "You were right."

Hope struggled to free herself from Charlotte's grasp.

"He was just helping, wasn't he?" Charlotte said, realizing she had murdered Drew out of anger and without justification. She was never really going to knife him, though she had insinuated that to Bob. She was only going to knock him out and tie him up. Killing someone was too much, even for her.

Hope tried to pry Charlotte's hand off her arm, but she couldn't, so she used the next best thing, her teeth. She bit down on Charlotte's knuckles.

"Aww, damn!" Charlotte cried.

The door to the room burst open, and Bob came rushing in. He opened his mouth to say something then paused when he saw Drew's body. "Oh, my God, you did it."

Hope sprinted past Bob and out the door.

"You really did it. Girl, you have bigger balls

than I do, that's for sure, but don't you think you could've waited? We're a bit ahead of schedule."

"Stop her," Charlotte hollered.

Hope raced out the front door and across the yard.

Charlotte followed, but Bob grabbed her from behind.

"Nope, you go out there and it's over. Once they find out you killed Drew, you'll be the main event in the fight tonight."

"Hope, we've got to get Hope," Charlotte bellowed.

"You'll thank me later, I promise."

"Hope, we have to get her!" Charlotte began to swing wildly.

A man entered from the far end of the building and called out, "Bob, what the hell is going on?"

Bob leaned in close to Charlotte and whispered, "Look what you've done."

The man walked past the girls' room and stopped when he saw the bloody mess and Drew's body. "What happened?"

"This little bitch, she killed him," Bob announced.

Charlotte began to kick and hit him. "You asshole."

The man headed for them, a look of rage on his face. "Well, well, looks like we have another contender for the fights tonight."

"No, you got it all wrong. He did it; Bob killed Drew. They were fighting over us," Charlotte declared.

The man stopped and gave Bob a suspicious look.

"You can't really think I would…"

"You are kind of a shit," the man said. "Let's see what Tony says. You both need to come with me."

Hope was stopped near the house. Her cries drew a small gathering of men.

Bob looked at the man, then Charlotte and then towards the group that was gathering outside the main house. He needed to act and act swiftly. "Listen, I didn't do a damn thing. I heard screaming and came over. I found Drew lying there just like you did."

The man took Bob by the arm and said, "Tony will decide who's telling the truth."

"You gotta believe me," Bob said.

"I've never believed a fucking word that's ever come out of your mouth from day one, Bob, if that's even your name. I could tell you weren't a chef from the first meal. Your cooking sucks."

"This little bitch did it," Bob pleaded.

"No, I didn't. He killed Drew, hoping to take us," Charlotte lied.

Panicked and afraid, Bob pushed the man away

and struck out with several punches to his face.

Stunned but able to fight back, the man hit Bob with several heavy punches to his stomach.

Bob keeled over and coughed.

The man then slammed an elbow into Bob's back, driving him to the floor.

Bob hacked and coughed. The hits had hurt, but he wasn't out of the fight. He grabbed the man by his legs and tackled him to the floor, then straddled him and began to pepper him with one punch after another.

Charlotte looked on in shock at the men fighting while simultaneously keeping a watchful eye on Hope and the group who stood encircling her.

Bob's relentless barrage of fists knocked the man out. Exhausted but proud of his victory, he rose and looked at Charlotte. "So you're trying to fuck me over?"

Charlotte turned to run.

Bob grabbed her by her long ponytail and yanked her back. Wrapping her hair around his hand, he slammed her against the wall and said, "You tried to fuck me over. Well, guess what? You fucked with the wrong person." He smashed her face against the wall.

The pain was agony. She had never experienced such pain before until Bob slammed her head again. She lost consciousness just after he did it a third time.

## CHAPTER TWELVE

"A leader is a dealer in hope." – Napoleon Bonaparte

### El Centro, CA

Neal's hand trembled as he leveled out the freshly dug dirt and patted it down. Sweat and tears dripped from his nose and chin onto the dry earth. As his hand hovered over the dirt, he picked rocks from the dirt and tossed them aside. It had to be perfect, he thought.

He paused when the shadow of a large falcon cast down. Looking up, he saw the majestic bird and smiled. "Will you watch over them?"

The falcon seamlessly coursed through the air. For it, the world was no different than it had always been. It went about its days unencumbered by the blackout that had swept the world he knew into chaos and then collapse.

Fatigue overcame him. Letting gravity work, he sat back heavily and watched the falcon coast; its dark brown feathers provided a contrast to the deep blue southern California sky. A partial grin cracked his bearded face as he continued to think about the bird and its life. He watched until the falcon soared over the neighboring houses and disappeared.

A gentle breeze washed over him and brought

with it the smell of dirt. This brought him back to his reality. Neal's reality for the past eight months had been nothing short of harrowing. He and his family had survived the initial riots and civil unrest brought on by the blackout, as it had been called. Living in the desert one hundred and eighteen miles east of San Diego gave them immunity from the large-scale troubles, but they still had their own, but none of that mattered now. The fighting, scavenging, and bare-knuckle survival he had dealt with for his family meant nothing anymore. All the work he had done to ensure they would be okay, all the preparations he had made were for naught without his wife and daughter. The question that kept plaguing him was, was it all worth going forward? What was the purpose of life if you didn't have someone to share it with? The times were hard enough, but before he had purpose, he had them, but in an instant they were taken from him.

Using what little strength he had, he got to his feet and brushed the dirt off his sweat-dampened clothes. There was more work to be done, but he dreaded the thought. Making burial markers for his wife and daughter was something that needed to be done, so he fought the desire to ignore it.

Over and over again he replayed when the first symptoms hit them. The dizziness, followed by the slurred speech and crushing fatigue, along with body aches drove them all to their beds, each unable to help the other. Like a skipping record, he repeated the peaches, the peaches, the damn peaches. He didn't recall Karen or Beth complaining that they tasted bad, but he had only consumed a small amount. Was that the reason he suffered less? He didn't have a formal diagnosis; without a professional opinion he'd never know for sure. Whatever it was that killed his family didn't matter; it hit them all like a semi-truck going a hundred and kept going.

There were stories of people losing time when something traumatic occurred. When his mind stopped wandering, he realized twelve hours had slipped by in almost an instant.

The idea of killing himself came right away, but he paused. They needed to be buried. He couldn't have their bodies lie; they had to be buried. He lifted his body off the ground, grabbed the shovel, and went back to shoveling.

Another three hours passed in a flash, but it was over finally. They were buried with markers at the heads of their graves. Neal looked towards the horizon to see the sun closing in on the mountains to the west. Would that be his last sunset? He turned and looked at the graves. Tears formed in his eyes and slid gently down his cheeks and into his beard.

Determined to let it all go, he walked back into

the house.

Inside, he saw the culprit. Jars of unopened peaches sat where they had been last placed by Karen after finding them in the SUV. He cleared the few steps towards the table and in a rage swept the jars off the table. They shattered into a thousand pieces on the tile floor. "Arghh!" he screamed.

Vertigo hit him hard. He fell into a chair and rested his head on the table.

A rush of tears came. "Why, God, why?"

His despair gave way to anger. He lifted his weary head and screamed, "Why, God? What kind of God allows this to happen? All of the death. Why my family? Why my baby girl? What had she done? She was only eight years old! She was innocent! Damn you, God, damn you!" He stood up and raced towards his office.

The fatigue was crushing, but he made it to the desk chair and plopped down. On his desk was his Sig. He picked it up and cradled it in his hand; his thumb ran over the slide. More tears came down his face. Slowly he raised the pistol and placed it under his chin. His hands shook as he placed his index finger on the trigger. The tears were gushing from his eyes. He gazed up at the ceiling, closed his eyes, and applied pressure to the trigger.

Karen's voice screamed in his head. The promise he had made her echoed over and over.

He kept applying pressure.

Now he could see her in his mind's eye, lying in the bed, making him swear to live on and help others.

Tears kept streaming down his face. He thought it impossible to cry any more. *How much can someone possibly cry?*

Again she came to him. He could almost feel her presence in the room. Having the feeling she was watching him do this cowardly act embarrassed him. Unable to go through with it, he lowered the pistol, looked at it and angrily tossed it away.

He made a promise and he was going to fulfill it. Looking up again, he shouted, "Fine, I won't do it. I won't, but there better be something greater out there. I'll do what you wish. I'll honor your dying wish and not take my own life, but you better be right because living seems fruitless. There's no meaning, there's nothing for me here, but I'll go forth. I love you, Karen. I love you, Beth."

Pine Valley, CA

Charlotte's head pounded and her body felt like it had been dragged for miles because it had. After knocking her out, Bob picked Charlotte up and fled the compound. The alarm Hope had sounded provided him a greater distraction than the Friday fights.

The perimeter guard, an undisciplined knuckle dragger, left his post to go see what the commotion was all about.

The guard's dereliction allowed Bob to escape with Charlotte. He tossed her over his shoulder and easily slipped through the fence line and down the hillside.

Many miles and hours were now in between her and Hope. What plans she thought she had yesterday were gone. In an instant it had all changed, and why? Because she had misjudged a situation and acted foolishly. How would she get back to Hope? How would she escape Bob?

"My stomach is growling," Bob complained.

Charlotte didn't respond. She sat in a patch of tall dry grass, with her hands bound behind her.

"You're a stupid fucking girl, you know that? You screwed this whole thing up."

"You told me he liked young girls. So when I found him and her, I thought he was doing something to her."

"Pretty boy Drew never touched a young girl; I just told you that to give you a reason to run away."

"You lied?"

"Boy, you're dumb."

"Why? Why did you need me and Hope to go with you? You could leave at anytime."

"I had thought about it for a while, but I knew I'd be walking out with nothing of value. Cash money is worthless, and unless you have a cache of guns, ammo or food, you're pretty much broke. Nope, couldn't happen. I waited for a sign for something to come and show me the timing was right, and guess what? You two girls come along. I said to myself, *Bob, that's your ticket right there.*"

"You didn't need us. I don't understand."

"Did I hit you too hard on the head, or are you really stupid?"

Charlotte's blood rose and her temper flared. "I should've put the knife in you. Had I known, I would've killed you."

"There's that fighting spirit again. You may be dumb as a sack of bricks, but you definitely have a fiery spirit."

Charlotte leered at him; her nostrils flared in anger.

Bob looked around, the sun was setting. He liked the idea of traveling under the concealment of night. "C'mon, get your little ass up. Time to go."

"Where are you taking me?"

"We're going to ole Mexico first."

Charlotte realized she needed to at least ask for mercy. "Please let me go. My sister, she's only six years old. She needs me."

"Your sister is probably dead by now, best you

forget about her," Bob said, deliberately being cruel.

Hearing that made Charlotte's stomach churn. "You're a monster."

Bob stopped, grabbed her firmly, and pulled her close. "I'm not a monster, I'm a survivor. And look at you, covered in blood. You call me a monster. You killed someone," Bob said, reminding her that she was capable of barbarism as much as anyone.

"I thought he was hurting her."

"You took joy in it, I saw you."

"I did not."

"You're the monster, not me."

Charlotte knew she had to remain calm so she could try to persuade him, but again her temper was her worst enemy. She spit in his face and yelled, "I hate you."

Bob wiped the spit from his face and drew his hand back to smack her but stopped just short of doing it.

"Go ahead, hit me," she taunted.

"No, I can't. I want to, but I need you looking pretty."

Charlotte feared that comment. *What did he mean?* she thought. "What are you going to do with me?" she asked.

"You're my currency. I can't damage my goods."

"What are you doing with me?" she again asked.

"I'm going to sell you to the highest bidder the

second I cross over into Mexico. They pay good money for white girls," he said with a grin.

## El Centro, CA

There were promises made, and Neal was about to fulfill one of those. He had found some time to rest, and it did make him feel better.

He put on a change of clothes, brushed his teeth, trimmed his beard, and even combed his thick hair back only to cover it with a ball cap. Once dressed, he put on his tactical vest, holstered his pistol, and inspected the magazines, ensuring they were fully loaded. As he walked to the front door, he grabbed his rifle and exited his house.

It was night, but he knew every step he'd have to take to get to where he was going.

One thing he loved about the desert was the cool but dry evenings. The temperature during the day could be in the high eighties or low nineties but dip into the sixties at night. And then there was the night sky. When the moon was riding high, the stars shined with brilliance. This was a favorite sight of his and something he loved to share with Beth.

Now he felt the cool air and looked up to see the stars dazzling, but the joy was lost on him. He felt numb, cold emotionally. Unless you'd lost someone close, it was hard to describe what he was feeling.

He began his short sojourn towards Felicia's house and was surprised how he felt once he made the first block. His body and health were returning. He hated that. He wished the botulism had taken him too.

The three-block walk ended with him standing in front of Felicia's house. Neal was instantly taken back to the day he was sitting on the front porch with Beth. How funny that in such a short period of time she was gone. How could that be? It all seemed so weird.

He knew what he'd encounter upon entering the house. He could see it already. There wasn't any doubt she was dead, probably lying in her bed. He just couldn't imagine a situation where she'd be alive. She was too old and frail to have survived to this point.

Even though he knew what was inside, he still had to go check. It was a promise he'd made to Karen, and not to do it would violate that pledge. However, what was stopping him was exactly the fact he'd have to see her corpse and have to go through with burying her.

He took a deep breath and took the necessary steps to clear the stairs. He stopped at the front door and paused. "It's going to reek in there," he said. In his left cargo pocket he pulled out a large black bandana and tied it around his face.

Satisfied that the smell of death would be kept to a minimum, he entered the house.

Even with the bandana, a putrid smell seeped through. He stopped and readjusted the bandana, but there was no way he could tie it tighter. Instead he began to breathe through his mouth. Unable to see, he turned on his LED headlamp. The bright white light illuminated the living room.

"Felicia?" he called out even though he knew he wouldn't get a reply.

He walked into the kitchen and looked around. Sitting on the counter was the empty jar of peaches. On the small dinette table three bowls with spoons were in the exact spots where they had been left by Felicia, Karen and Beth. Seeing them made him heartsick as he thought about the last time they had been used. It was all so sad.

From the kitchen he entered the short hallway.

"Felicia?" he again called out.

He passed the other rooms and went directly to the master bedroom. He walked through the open door, and there on the bed was Felicia. It appeared she had managed to change her clothes from that day, but the evidence of food poisoning was everywhere.

He approached the side of the bed and thought about how he'd remove her so he could bury her. He'd rather not, but if he didn't, he just knew Karen would haunt him.

He untucked the sheet and mattress cover and pulled it over her. Dreading what he was about to do, he took a few deep breaths, put on a pair of gloves, and once he'd found the courage, he bent over and ran his arms under her body so he could lift her up.

With his arms under her, he noticed she wasn't cold like he expected.

Her body moved, startling him.

He put her back down quickly and focused his light on her face.

Her eyes were open but not glazed over like he'd seen before on corpses. Ever so slightly she lifted her arm.

She was alive!

"Felicia, um, you're alive?" he said, shocked.

She opened her mouth a sliver, but nothing came out. Her arm again rose but dropped right away.

"Let me help you. Have you eaten, drank? Yes, you need to drink water. You're dehydrated. Let me get you some water," Neal said, the beam from his headlamp darting around the room as he looked everywhere for water close by. "I'll be right back."

"No," she said, barely audible.

He stopped and looked back at her.

"No."

"Felicia, let me help you," Neal insisted.

She slowly shook her head.

"All you need is water and more rest. I managed to survive and maybe you can too."

"Karen?" she asked.

Neal's frantic behavior stopped when she asked for Karen. He lowered his head and replied, "She and Beth didn't make it."

Her hand crawled along the sheet until it found his dangling arm. She touched him and said, "Die."

"Yes, they died."

"Die, me."

"No, you won't, not if I can help it," Neal said, the urgency coming back.

"No, me, die, please."

Neal was on his way out the door when he heard her. He turned and asked, "Are you asking me not to help you?"

"Die."

Neal walked to her side and sat down. "Are you really asking me to let you just die? I can't do that, I can't."

She was weak, barely able to talk, but found the energy to clearly state her desires by showing him. Her thin and shaking arm grabbed a pillow and pulled it over her face.

He looked at her strangely for a second; then it dawned on him what she was asking. He recoiled at the suggestion. "No, I can't, I won't."

She removed the pillow, opened her eyes and

said, "Please."

"No."

She reached for him and touched his leg.

Neal jumped and walked away from the bed. "No, what you're asking me to do…I can't do that." Disturbed and upset, he stormed out of the room and went outside. He ripped the headlamp off his head and sat down on the same steps he'd sat on with Beth that fateful day.

His mind spun with how he would handle this situation. *Am I capable of killing her?* he asked himself. He had killed before, but just recently, and that still freaked him out. However, killing two people intent on killing you was different than this. He understood the concept of mercy killing, but he knew Felicia. She was a good friend and motherly figure to Karen and treated Beth like her own granddaughter. Doing what she asked was like killing his own family member, something he had trouble seeing himself do.

An hour went by in a flash as he struggled with the decision. He had three choices. He could just leave her to die naturally, he could attempt to nurse her back to health only to fail, or he could go in there and end her suffering. She clearly wanted to die, so any attempt to nurse her would be futile and only prolong her suffering. You couldn't force people to eat or drink, and if her will to live wasn't there, she would just die anyway—again taking him back to his first choice, just leaving. He began to weigh that option. If he just left, she'd die but suffer, and he'd fail as a friend and fail Karen's dying wish to help people, but was killing Felicia by suffocating her *helping?* Would Karen support that? He looked up and asked, "What would you do? Huh, tell me."

Another hour slipped by as he sat debating the issue. Maybe he'd go in and find her dead. He'd be off the hook, but she would have suffered waiting for his return. One thing he couldn't escape was how he felt about himself. It was a reoccurring word that kept taunting him over and over. Was he a coward? Was he to blame for everything? Was it his inability to help Carlos that led to all of this? Was he now acting like a coward, unable to give a person he cared about her dying wish? If she wanted to die, shouldn't he allow her that last bit of dignity, shouldn't he allow her to have control over her last moments? Who was he to refuse that?

The answer finally came to him. He had wasted too much of her time and his.

With renewed confidence, he went to her bedside.

She opened her eyes just above a slit and looked at him.

"Karen and Bethie love you so much. You are a great woman and were a great friend to them. Thank you so much," he said.

She touched his arm.

He didn't recoil this time; instead he took her small hand in his.

She rolled her head and closed her eyes.

Neal grabbed the pillow, and without hesitation he covered her face and pushed down hard. Tears welled up in his eyes as he counted down. He didn't know why he was doing that, but it seemed natural to have an idea of how long he was suffocating her.

Tears fell from his nose and chin onto the pillow. "Ninety-nine, one hundred," he said, then lifted the pillow off her face and checked her pulse and found nothing. She was dead, and by his hand.

Neal carried her wrapped in her sheets and placed her in the shallow grave he'd dug in her backyard.

He grabbed the shovel and was about to toss the first shovelful of dirt when he remembered her husband. Neal put the shovel down and went back into the house. On the mantel, a large stainless urn sat. He picked it up and said, "Let's have you two rest together." Cradling the urn, he took it outside and placed it next to Felicia and began the process of covering her up.

It was a well-known fact to his friends that Neal wasn't religious although he was raised Baptist, but Felicia was a devoted Catholic, so he felt it necessary to say a prayer. He bowed his head and recited the

Lord's Prayer. When he finished, he said, "I can't believe I remembered that." He exited the house via the side gate and somberly walked back home in deep thought over what had just occurred. In his years of being alive he had never harmed anyone. In fact, he had only been in two fistfights. Now within the span of a week he had killed three people.

## CHAPTER THIRTEEN

"Where there is no vision, there is no hope." – George Washington Carver

Ten Miles Southeast of Pine Valley, CA

Bob wrapped his legs around the man and tightened the strap around his neck.

The man gagged and frantically grasped at his neck in a desperate attempt to loosen Bob's hold, but it wasn't working.

Bob knew he had him; all he had to do was hold on. With all his might he squeezed hard and pulled back with all his weight.

The man's eyes were bulging, and he turned blue, then snap. His head fell forward.

Bob not only felt it but heard the man's neck breaking. He let go of the strap, rolled off the man and hooted loudly. "Hot damn, that motherfucker was big."

Charlotte stepped towards him, a large wrench in her hand.

"Look at you." Bob laughed. He got to his knees and said, "Well, come on, try to escape again. Go for it, and I'll just knock you on your ass like I did ten minutes ago." Bob was referencing Charlotte's unsuccessful attempt to escape after they encountered the now dead man and his family on the road. Bob looked and saw the wife and two young kids were gone. He smirked and asked, "Did you let them go?"

"Yes."

He got to his feet, dusted himself off and asked, "The question is why didn't you run off too? I'm over here battling it out with this fucking giant of a man and you could have bailed. Why?"

"Because I'm going to kill you!" Charlotte barked and lunged at him.

He easily pushed her to the ground.

She got to her feet and came at him again.

He stepped aside and pushed her down.

She fell hard on the gravel shoulder of the highway.

"Charlotte, you let your anger get in your way. You could've run, but nope, you got so mad that you thought it best to get revenge. You wasted that attempt just so you could try to kill me. What a stupid girl."

"I hate you!" she yelled. She had thought about running, but the urge to see him die trumped her desire to escape.

"Now get up and get your ass in the truck. I don't want to be sitting on the side of a highway forever."

"No," she said, scrambling to her feet and

sprinting away.

"Really? Now you're just going to piss me off," Bob said, chasing after her.

Charlotte darted up an embankment but slid down and into Bob's grasp. He wrapped his arm around her throat and put her in a rear naked choke hold.

She punched and kicked, but it was no use.

"Say goodnight," Bob said as he squeezed hard.

Charlotte struggled for a second before blacking out.

He carried her to the truck and put her in. Before shutting the door, he bound her arms and legs and put duct tape over her mouth from a roll he found under the seat.

"I thought we worked like a good team there, well, up until you opened your stupid mouth and warned those people. You know I blame you for him dying," Bob said, rambling out loud as he gestured towards the dead man behind him. "All you had to do was keep your mouth shut; I didn't want to kill that guy. Nope, all I wanted to do was steal their truck. We were a good team for a second; you had that sweet girl, 'I need help' look, and I show up and take the truck. Nope, no, no, you had to go do that. And the kids, you also cost me; those kids would have been perfect to sell." He finished his last knot and shoved her over so he could close the door.

"You're more of a pain in the ass than you're worth, but soon enough I'll be rid of you. Now that I got a truck, all I need is food, and you'll buy me quite a bit, yep, you will."

"This is not my day!" Bob yelled, gripping the steering wheel with white knuckles.

The truck swerved hard left, then right.

Charlotte's head smacked against the side of the door, waking her. She sat up as best she could considering her hands and feet were bound.

Bob was struggling to get the truck under control.

Charlotte didn't know what was happening as she watched in fear as the truck surged hard left.

Bob lifted his foot off the accelerator to help slow the speed and gently tamped on the brakes.

Two abandoned cars sat on the road ahead, and with nature slowly retaking the road, it didn't leave Bob with anywhere to go except in the ditch.

He cranked the wheel hard to the right, just avoiding one car only to have the right wheels slip into the ditch and clip a boulder.

The force from the impact only slowed them.

Feeling safe to hit the brakes fully, Bob pressed down hard until the truck came to a full stop.

Charlotte mumbled, but was unintelligible with the duct tape on her mouth.

"Damn!" Bob yelled. He looked at her and barked, "Just shut up."

She did as he said.

He got out and began to look for any damage beyond the left rear tire, which had blown, sending them on a wild ride.

Charlotte sat and waited.

"Well, it all looks okay. I think all I need to do is put the spare on and we'll be on the road again." He looked in the bed but didn't see the spare there, so he looked under the bed. Nothing there either. "Well, what do you know? No spare. Isn't that a son of a bitch?"

Charlotte sighed when she heard the news. Anything that would slow their trip to Mexico gave her more time to escape. Next time she would just run, or that was what she told herself.

Bob looked at the two cars he had barely missed and surmised the small tires from the compact cars wouldn't work.

Heavy steam suddenly appeared from under the hood.

Bob saw it and yelled, "Are you fucking kidding me?" He reached in the truck, popped the hood latch and opened the hood to discover a large dried timber had pierced the grill and a radiator hose. "Looks like we're down for a bit until I can get it fixed."

Charlotte mumbled loudly.

"What?"

She mumbled again.

Irritated, he reached in and forcefully yanked the tape from her mouth.

"Ouch!"

"What?"

"I have to pee."

"Then go pee."

She nodded to her legs and arms.

"Scoot over," he ordered.

She did as he said and he untied her.

"Now don't go acting stupid. I'm not in the mood."

Charlotte was always thinking about hurting him and escaping, she just needed to prioritize the escape versus the hurt.

She slid out of the driver's side, as the passenger door was blocked, and walked to the back and squatted to pee.

Bob looked at the damage then caught sight that the right front tire looked odd. He bent down and looked in the wheel well to discover the axle rod was snapped. "Fuck! That's it. We're screwed. It's back to walking. We don't have water, food, nothing, and now the truck is ruined. Shit!" He picked up a rock and threw it hard.

Charlotte finished and walked to the cab. She hid her joy at the news, knowing that could potentially enrage him. "What now?"

"We walk," Bob said.

"But it's—"

"Just shut your mouth. I'm in charge," Bob said. He looked down the road to get his bearings and continued, "We're getting close to the desert; see how the topography is changing. We definitely went quite a few miles. Luckily for us, it's all downhill from here. There's an old gas station at the base of the mountain near Ocotillo."

"There won't be anything there," Charlotte said.

"I said shut your mouth," Bob snapped, fully knowing she was right.

Charlotte folded her arms and stared at him.

"Those cars, we go check those cars for anything of value," Bob said, pointing to the two compact cars.

"Okay," Charlotte said as she turned and began to walk that way.

"Hold on. You're coming with me, but there's no way I'm letting you scavenge with me. I'm not stupid," he said, getting the rope and tying her hands together but this time behind her back.

"Aren't you going to put the tape on my mouth?" she quipped.

"You know, I just might if you keep that mouth running."

Charlotte smiled, she just couldn't resist. She was

a sassy tween girl with an attitude, but if she couldn't get her anger in check, she just might end up dead.

## El Centro, CA

Neal pulled everything he thought he could use out of his and Carlos' houses. He stood and looked over the heap of things and wondered if his next move was the right one. He didn't want to leave the home he had shared with Karen and Beth, but he couldn't stay either. His life was over there, but where would he go was the question. Alaska came to mind, as that was the final destination the group had decided on, but was that where he wanted to go now?

He backed up and sat on the curb. His body ached and his legs were weak. Every hour that went by, he felt better, but he definitely wasn't a hundred percent physically.

The sun had set over the mountains, and soon he'd be wrapped in the black of night. He couldn't find it in him to sleep another night at the house, so his mind was set on that account.

Tired, he lay back on the cool cement and looked up. *Where should I go? What would Karen want?* he asked himself. His mind raced through destinations, and none felt right. He pressed his eyes closed and asked out loud, "Where do you want me to go, Karen? Where? Please tell me, give me a sign, something."

Random images came, but he felt like he was forcing those, so he calmed his breathing and tried to meditate.

The random images of the mountains gave way to clear visions of a beach, palm fronds and the ocean. He struggled to find out specifically where that was. Frustrated, he opened his eyes and grumbled, "Where is that?"

Knowing he wouldn't get the answer if he forced it, he again closed his eyes and cleared his thoughts.

The images of a beach and ocean again came, but they were brighter than before. He saw the ocean lapping the shores of the beach, and off in the distance he saw a sailboat.

He sat up and blurted out, "The sailboat. Is that what you want? That makes sense; you want me to go to the sailboat. You want me to find Kate and sail away."

He stood up and began to prep for his impending departure. He had the clarity he needed; he was sure that this was it. He knew the journey would be dangerous, long, and he might never find Kate, but he had a purpose, he had something that gave him a reason to wake each day going forward.

The beam from his headlamp cast the bright LED light on his new mode of transportation, a Kona mountain bike. Attached to the rear spoke was the old baby trailer Beth rode in when she was a toddler. He'd use it now to tow all the food, water and gear he'd need for the trip. With few routes to take west, his plan had him going along Interstate 8 and traveling mostly at night. The initial miles west would be fairly easy, as he'd be riding along the flat desert; however, the mountains to the west would not be easy, so he calculated his trip would take longer just because of the terrain and his weakened condition. But did it matter when he got there? No, it didn't, he just liked to have plans.

With the bike and trailer ready, he was ready to commit to his last act at the house.

He and Carlos had stockpiled gallons of gasoline in a shed off the back of Carlos' house. Once again wrapping the bandanna around his face, he entered Carlos's house. It swarmed with hordes of flies. They buzzed loudly and filled the windows. The large brown stains marking the dying place of his friends were covered in humming insects. He pulled the cap from one of the cans and began to douse everything in both homes. He couldn't quite peg why he thought it important to do so; he just didn't want anyone to have anything from it or to enter and disrespect the things he and his family once cherished. Maybe it was the way those men had trashed Carlos' house that he knew most people just didn't care, so to leave it for others to ransack wasn't an option. He had control over what happened to the stuff, and he was going to burn it all to the ground.

Maybe this exercise was more about cleansing rather than control. But did it matter? Not to Neal it didn't.

He poured a trail of gasoline out to the center of the cul-de-sac and tossed the gas can. Knowing how volatile gasoline and the fumes could be, he stepped back to a safe distance. In his right hand Neal held a classic Zippo lighter that Carlos' father had passed down. Carlos commented on it every time he proudly lit it to share a Cuban cigar with friends. Now Neal would use it one last time. He flicked it open and lit it. The orange flame danced to the subtle air movements. He watched and thought of those special moments with his friend. How they'd laughed and joked as well as shared moment's only dear friends could. His thoughts then drifted to Karen and Beth and the memories this house held for them. He found himself going back and forth as to destroying the homes, but he just couldn't imagine them rotting. No, he needed this. He needed to have a sense of control over this.

He tossed the lighter onto the trail of gasoline.

The second the Zippo landed, the trail of gas erupted.

Neal watched in amazement as the fiery trail split

and went to both houses. When it entered the homes almost simultaneously, the houses roared to life in spectacular fashion. The fires quickly engulfed the homes with flames licking every crevice.

The heat that came from the homes was intense, forcing Neal to step back further. Unexpectedly flames jumped to the neighbor's house next to Carlos', and in seconds that house was on fire.

"Well, shit, isn't that something." Neal laughed as the house next to his caught fire too.

With four homes ablaze, Neal thought it best to leave. Not only would he draw attention to himself, he didn't want to be stuck in the middle of an inferno.

He stepped on the bike and pedaled to the end of the street. He stopped and turned to see two more homes had caught. He chuckled and rode off, singing an old Bloodhound Gang song.

## CHAPTER FOURTEEN

"Hope, deceiving as it is, serves at least to lead us to the end of our lives by an agreeable route." – Francois de La Rochefoucauld

### Ocotillo, CA

Neal shoved the bicycle and cursed, "Argh, fuck!" He had ridden thirty, maybe forty miles, and just when he thought things were going well, he dozed off and crashed the bike. After picking himself up, he examined the bike and breathed a sigh of relief when he found it still operable. Nothing could be worse for him but to break the bike so many miles from San Diego.

The sun would be rising soon, and the last place he wanted to be was on the road in broad daylight, hiking in the heat.

A couple hundred yards on the right side of the interstate, he saw an outcropping of rocks. There he'd get good cover and shade. He could push the bike and the trailer that far and settle down for a good nap.

Neal swore the rock outcropping was a quarter mile away, but as he took each step, he realized he had sorely underestimated the distance. The desert had a way of fooling you.

"Damn," he grunted. Tired and thirsty, he stopped and pulled a bottle of water from the trailer. Surprisingly the water was staying cool in the covered trailer.

"Hey you, mister!" a man hollered in the distance.

Neal turned quickly, spilling his water, and looked for the source of the voice.

"Mister, help!" the man hollered.

Untrusting of anyone, Neal dropped the water bottle and pulled out his Sig.

The man waved his arms and again cried out, "Please help. We're hungry and thirsty."

"We're? Who's with you?" Neal asked in reply to the man.

As if on cue, a young girl appeared from a culvert on the eastbound lanes.

"Don't come any closer, please!" Neal ordered, still maintaining a bit of civility with his use of polite words.

They kept waving their arms and yelling, "Please help us, please!"

Neal kept his pistol at the ready but didn't raise it. He stood his ground and waited.

The man and young girl kept walking towards him.

"Just hold it right there," Neal ordered.

The man did as he was told and froze in his

tracks. The girl two steps behind followed suit. They were fifty feet from Neal in the center of the highway's median.

"Where you coming from?" Neal asked.

"West of here, near San Diego," the man replied.

"This your daughter?" Neal asked.

The man looked at the girl and back to Neal. "Um, no, she's a niece. She's my niece."

"Where you heading?" Neal asked.

"Mexico, but does it matter, mister? We need some food and water. Please help us," the man pleaded.

The girl remained quiet, her head down.

"You…girl, what say you?" Neal asked, noticing she seemed distracted or adrift mentally.

"Huh?" she asked, lifting her head.

"Are you okay?" Neal asked.

The girl just stood there, her stare telling Neal she was not quite right.

"Answer him!" the man barked.

"I'm fine."

"C'mon, mister, we need some help. Can you spare a bit of food and drink?" the man asked.

"Where are your weapons?" Neal asked.

"All I have is a pistol and a knife."

"You'll understand if I ask you to put your gun on the ground and step away from it."

"I don't think I can do that. I'm just as skeptical

as you are of me but not too scared to ask for a bit of food and drink. If I put my only means of defense down, who says you don't kill me and take the girl," the man said.

"Then move on. I don't have time to negotiate my safety with a stranger," Neal said.

Recognizing Neal held all the cards, the man said, "How about this? You grab some food, lay it on the ground with a bottle of water, and go about your business? You move on and we go get what you left after you're well clear of us."

Neal thought about it. He couldn't really spare any food or water considering his trip would now take longer. However, Karen's voice rang in his head to help those in need.

"How about it?" the man asked.

Neal thought. He didn't want to, but what would Karen do?

The girl wobbled and fell to her knees hard.

"Get up," the man barked.

She tried to stand, but gravity and whatever ailed her took over. She fell onto her side and lay there.

Neal took a few steps towards them but hesitated when the man turned and grabbed the girl by the arm.

"Get up," the man snapped.

"Ease up on her. She's clearly worn out," Neal said.

"You see, we need water and some food. It's been days since we drank," the man said and pulled the girl up.

"I'll tell you what; I'll leave some food and a couple bottles of water here."

"Thank you."

Without taking his eyes off the man, Neal reached into the trailer and pulled out several packets of tuna, a packet of saltines and two bottles of water. He set them on the ground and said, "Here you go. Now I suggest you get off the road before daylight hits. It's safer to travel at night."

"Um, I see you're heading west," the man suggested.

"Maybe."

"Hey, I don't give a hoot where you're going; just giving you a heads-up is all."

"Why?"

"Well, if you're going past the casino, I'd take a different route," the man warned.

"And why?"

"The feds have roadblocks and a camp near there."

"And?"

"It just doesn't look too safe around there. If you have another route, I'd take it," the man said.

"I'll keep that in mind," Neal said as he holstered his pistol and began his trek towards the rock outcropping.

Neal kept a careful eye on the two strangers. He watched them cross the road after he was well past. They dove into the food and ate ravenously.

He was cautious, but if there was a God, and needless to say he was having his doubts, his actions today would go a long way to helping him get past the pearly gates when it was his time. He already had to ration his food, but knowing Karen was looking down on him with pride helped make the decision easier.

He finally reached the safety of the rocks and set up camp under a large overhang. He inspected the spot for rattlesnakes or any other critters and laid out a tarp and put down his sleeping bag.

Like stray dogs, the two strangers headed towards him. He just hoped they weren't the feral type.

"Stop right there," Neal ordered.

Like before, they stopped.

"I wanted to thank you," the man said.

"Thank you," the girl said in her timid voice.

"You're welcome. Now move on. I did my nice deed for today."

"We thought maybe we could share some conversation," the man said.

Neal didn't like the situation and said, "No, now

move on."

"Don't be a jerk," the man barked.

"Jerk? I gave you some food and water, and now all I ask for in return is some privacy," Neal insisted.

"Well, you don't own the world. We're going to set up over here," the man said as he and the girl marched towards another outcropping of boulders some twenty feet from Neal.

"Damn it," Neal said under his breath. He didn't like people close by, and how was he going to sleep knowing they were a stone's throw away. He watched as they headed away, the girl trailing the man like before. The backpack that hung from her shoulders looked empty. Her arms dangled and barely moved as she shuffled. She looked weary and defeated to him.

The girl and her tattered appearance pulled at Neal's heartstrings. He wondered what horrors she had witnessed. No doubt being on the road was difficult for an adult much less a child.

"We'll camp right here, next to our new friend," the man said as they walked off.

The girl said nothing. She opened her right hand, which had been fisted, and dropped a crumpled piece of paper. When it hit the ground, she turned and looked to see if Neal saw.

He was watching.

When they locked eyes, she nodded.

Neal wasn't an expert in body language but could tell that was a signal. He jumped to his feet and cleared the distance to retrieve the paper. He unfolded it to find two words handwritten: *HELP ME*.

Alarmed by the note, he lifted his gaze and watched as the man and girl settled in. Neal's heart pounded heavy in his chest. With this knowledge could he just walk away or do nothing? Was it a ruse to get him close so they could attack him and take his stuff? Dozens of scenarios played out in his thoughts.

The man barked orders to the girl, who obeyed without question.

He needed to process this possible development. There wasn't a clock ticking on when he acted, but if it were true, he needed to help, but just how he'd do that was the unknown equation.

Neal's eyes grew heavy, but each time before they closed, he'd open them wide and readjust his sitting position. He had come to the decision to act, but each time he thought about how, he'd hesitate. The problem with hesitation was he needed to sleep. Knowing the man not twenty-five feet from him couldn't be trusted made the timeline short.

He punched his thigh hard to stay awake. He played out exactly how he saw the encounter going.

He'd walk over, pull his pistol on the man, and demand the girl be released. The man would comply and leave peacefully. Problem solved. No altercation and everyone could go their own way, only he would have a new traveling companion.

Neal's head dropped. He had fallen asleep again. This time he stood to wake himself. He paced his small campsite. Over and over he ran through what he was going to do. He'd gather the nerve to walk over and confront the man, but he'd suddenly stop as a contrary thought would trump it.

"Get it together," he chided himself.

Was it the fatigue that was causing him pause, or was he scared? Was that it, was he a coward? He hadn't gone to help Carlos because of fear. He had convinced himself and told Karen that it was more about them than him, but was that even true? He hated confrontation, but maybe deep down he was nothing but a spineless coward.

The man yelled something unintelligible.

Neal turned and saw him jabbing his finger in the girl's face.

"Do it," Neal said under his breath. He began his march towards the man and girl, his fists clenched and his eyes fixed squarely on the man.

"Hey there, come and join us," the man said, waving Neal over with a crooked smile.

Neal stopped feet from their makeshift campsite

and bluntly asked, "Who are you?"

"I'm no one, just a weary traveler on this long road. I'm no different than you. I'm looking for a better place, a safe place for me and my niece."

The girl looked up at Neal.

Neal caught her staring; he returned her look then trained his eyes back on the man.

"What's going on here?" Neal asked.

"My friend, take a seat. Please, let's talk. You seem tired and, to be quite frank…agitated," the man said calmly, motioning with his hand for Neal to sit down.

"No."

"Then what can I do for you?" the man asked, his tone shifting to irritation.

Neal gulped; a bead of sweat coursed down his face. "This girl, you," Neal said, looking at the girl now, "are you here against your will?"

"Leave now. Thank you for your help earlier, but I can see you're nothing but trouble," the man said, his hand inching around behind him towards the pistol tucked in the waistband of his pants.

"Are you here against your will?" Neal asked the girl.

She sat motionless. Her facial muscles tightened and her eyes widened.

"Just tell me, it's fine," Neal said.

The man kept moving his right hand ever so

slowly.

Neal held up the piece of paper and said, "You dropped this."

The girl was rigid, her body frozen in fear.

The man placed his hand on the grip of his pistol and pulled it out swiftly.

Neal reacted, but his timing was off and he knew it the second it all went down.

The girl leaped on the man, forcing him to fall backwards.

A struggle ensued between the girl and the man.

Neal stepped forward to help when a shot rang out.

The girl rolled off the man. A patch of thick blood appeared on her shirt.

The man looked crazy eyed at Neal and swung his pistol towards him.

Neal, now ready, leveled his Sig and squeezed off two shots; both struck the man squarely in the chest.

The man looked down at the wounds in his chest, looked up at Neal and, with blood pouring from his mouth, muttered, "Would you fucking look at that." He coughed up more blood before slouching to his side and exhaling his last breath.

The girl scooted away from the man and nestled up against the jagged rocks. She placed her hand on the bloodstain and whimpered.

"Let me see the damage," he said, immediately

seeing to her.

The girl lifted her shirt, showing him the damage that was done. The bullet had ripped through her midsection just below her right ribs.

Neal rolled her gently to examine her back and found the bullet had exited. "It went through. That's good."

"Please help," she moaned.

"I will, I promise. I'll take care of you," he replied.

She began to cry and shake.

"I need you to remain calm. Sit tight. I'll be right back. I need to get my first aid kit," Neal said and sprinted towards his campsite. He tore through the trailer until he found it and raced back.

"Please help me, please," she begged, grabbing his arm.

Neal again reassured her, "I'll take care of you. Just sit still and let me clean you up. Breathe easy, take full and slow breaths."

She nodded.

Neal started addressing the wound.

She squinted as he wiped up the blood.

"You'll be fine, I promise."

She nodded.

"What's your name?"

The pain was becoming intense for her. She again grabbed his arm and squeezed.

## HOPE

"You've got a good grip there. My name is Neal. What's yours?"

"Help, please."

"I'm helping. I'll get this cleaned up, and then I'll need to—"

"My sister, you have to help my sister."

"Where's your sister? Is she close by?"

"Help my sister, you have to."

Neal didn't know why she was trusting him, but she was.

"I didn't get your name."

She cried out in pain.

"You'll be fine."

"Hope."

Neal wasn't focused on her face, so he didn't notice she had turned white and was going into shock.

"Hope, help," she mumbled. Her voice was becoming garbled.

"You hope I'll help. I am."

"No, Hope...sister."

"Oh, got it. Hope is your sister's name. What's your name, sweetheart?"

"Char..."

Hearing the way she responded, he looked at her face. "No, don't you dare die on me."

"I'm..."

Neal stopped working on her wound so he could

make sure she wasn't dying. He touched her face and could feel how cool her skin was.

When he touched her, she fully opened her eyes and looked at him. "Help, please."

"I am, but don't you dare die on me, okay?"

She nodded.

"Now just rest. I've got you. You're safe now."

She again nodded and closed her eyes.

"Char, hmm, let me guess. Charlie?"

She shook her head.

"Is your name Charlene?"

Again she shook her head.

"Darn," he joked. He was attempting to make her feel at ease with his banter, and it seemed to be working. "Oh, let me see, Char, Char, um, I give up," he said as he began stitching her abdomen.

"Charlotte."

"Charlotte! That's a beautiful name. And your sister is Hope?"

She didn't respond. Her head rolled gently to the side as she drifted off.

"You sleep. You're in good hands, I promise," Neal said. He looked up to the sky and said, "Are you seeing this, Karen, huh? Are you happy?"

## CHAPTER FIFTEEN

"Hope is being able to see that there is light despite all of the darkness." – Desmond Tutu

### Ocotillo, CA

Another day and another curveball had been hurled at Neal. He hadn't gone looking for trouble, but trouble found him. Now he was responsible for the care and well-being of Charlotte, whose wound was bad and her condition worsening.

Charlotte was awake and staring cautiously at Neal.

Not sure what to say, Neal asked, "How did you and your old traveling companion meet?"

"My sister and I were taken from our house."

"By that guy?"

"Not him, but he was part of that group."

Neal shook his head and thought, *What happens to men when they group up in an apocalypse?*

"He promised to help us."

"You keep mentioning your sister. Why isn't your sister with you?" he asked.

Not wanting to give away what specifically happened, Charlotte decided not to disclose all the information. "We got separated. I tried to go get her, but Bob took me."

"And for what purpose?"

"To sell me."

"I've heard it all now; he was going to sell you?"

"Yes. Don't you believe me?"

"I do. I have to say I'm just not shocked anymore. This world is upside down."

"You have to help me; you have to go get Hope."

Neal looked towards the sky and said, "Is this what you wanted?"

Charlotte looked at him oddly and asked, "Who are you talking to?"

"My wife."

Charlotte adjusted herself. She was lying on Neal's sleeping bag, but the hard ground was becoming uncomfortable, and her wounds were painful. "Can I have some aspirin or something?"

"I gave you some Advil and a hydrocodone, but I'm not sure about giving you anything more hardcore than that. Do you know if you're allergic to anything?"

"Not that I know of."

"If the pain becomes worse, I'll see what I can do."

"You have to go get my sister," Charlotte again insisted.

"Charlotte, I'll help you, I'll even help you find your sister, but we're not going anywhere anytime soon. You're hurt and you need to heal."

"Just leave me. Go, go now. She's only six; she needs me."

"I'm not leaving you here."

"Go, please."

"Get some more rest, and if you're better tomorrow, we'll set out," Neal said. He didn't know exactly how he would take her with him in her current condition. She had lost a lot of blood, and with his bike already difficult to ride because it was so heavy, he couldn't imagine putting her in there and making for San Diego or wherever her sister was. He could empty the bike of all the supplies, but that would be too risky.

He was in an almost impossible situation. Any way he looked at it, he didn't have enough food and water. In another week or less he'd run out and then what?

In some ways he welcomed the outcome with open arms if it led to his death. He could happily and peacefully die knowing he didn't take his own life, just so he could be reconnected with Karen and Beth. But was that possible? Was there an afterlife? This was where he became fearful of death. The possibility that there wasn't an afterlife, only darkness, struck fear within him. He wanted to have faith, but after all of his experiences, he struggled to believe. He wanted to have faith that there was a

God, but he couldn't help but ask what kind of God would allow such suffering. He was aware of all the debate and the rationale for free will, but didn't God provide miracles? Why didn't he come down and give mankind the biggest miracle since Jesus' resurrection? If he did, many people could have been saved and would still be alive. His struggles with believing were as real to him as his struggles to survive the drudgery of this new world.

"What happened to your wife?" Charlotte asked.

Neal couldn't hear her. His thoughts had drifted away.

"Your wife, what happened to her?" she asked again after clearing her throat loudly.

Jolted back to the present, Neal replied, "Oh, um, she died. My daughter died too."

"How?"

"Sick, they got really sick."

"I'm sorry."

"Me too," he said and chuckled.

"What's so funny?" she asked, finding his snicker odd.

"Our conversation, it's so weird. If someone asked me a year ago if I'd be sitting in the desert off the interstate, nursing a teenager with a bullet wound, and that my family would be dead and the world had gone crazy, I'd say that was an absurd situation, an impossible one. But look at us. It's real. You're here,

# HOPE

my family is dead, and I'm traveling to San Diego in hopes of sailing away on my boat after I help rescue a little girl named Hope."

"I guess it does sound weird."

Neal sighed loudly and rested against a large boulder.

"Where are you from?" she asked.

"El Centro."

"Before all of this, what did you do, for work, that is?"

"I drove trucks for a distribution company."

"Like the big ones, the tractor trailers?"

"Yeah, but I wasn't an over-the-road trucker."

"What's an over-the-road?"

"It's nothing," Neal replied, not wanting to have the conversation anymore.

Charlotte could tell he had pulled back.

"You need to rest."

"Okay," Charlotte said and closed her eyes.

Neal stretched out and tucked his backpack under his head.

"Thank you," Charlotte said.

"You're welcome," Neal replied.

"Goodnight," Charlotte said.

"Goodnight. Now get some rest," Neal said, hoping she'd be quiet.

Charlotte slowly drifted off.

Sleep sounded good, but Neal found it

impossible to shut his mind down. His thoughts bounced from Karen to Felicia to Charlotte then to Hope, the faceless little girl who needed to be rescued. It would be so easy to just leave Charlotte lying there and set out alone. He didn't need to do anything; he wasn't truly obligated. It would be so much easier to just ignore the suffering around him and head directly for the boat and set sail, leaving it all behind. But how could he live with that? Life wasn't easy nor was doing the right thing.

Beth came to mind. He posed the hypothetical question of her being alive and alone. Would he want someone like him to go save her? Of course he would. These two girls needed help, and for whatever reason, their salvation was put right in front of him. He had to see it through.

## CHAPTER SIXTEEN

*"All hope abandon, ye who enter here!"* – Dante Alighieri

### Ocotillo, CA

"Hope, no," Charlotte mumbled. Neal woke to find dawn had arrived. He had slept for hours, something he needed.

"Hope, please, no," Charlotte again mumbled. He looked over at her and saw her eyes were closed and her face glistened with a pasty sweat. She rocked her head back and forth while mumbling unintelligible gibberish.

Concerned, he rose and felt her skin. She was burning up. Overnight she had developed a fever, most likely from the wound. He lifted her shirt and instantly saw problem number one: her abdomen was enlarged, bloated and blue. He pulled the bandage back, and blood mixed with pus oozed from the stitching. Red striations jetted out from the hole, also signaling that the wound was festering.

Neal wasn't good at medical care past first aid, but he could tell she had two problems that could be fatal. First, she had internal bleeding, and second, she had an infection.

"Charlotte, you hear me?" he asked.

She opened her eyes and answered, "Yes."

"I'm not going to sugarcoat this, but you're in bad shape."

She pressed her eyes closed, took a deep breath, and licked her lips.

"Did you hear me?"

"Yes," she replied.

He thought that maybe he needed to drain the wound, but he didn't know. Where was a doctor or someone skilled in medical care when you needed one? Like before with Karen and Beth, he regretted never getting any training. He just never imagined he'd ever be in this type of situation, yet here he was, unprepared with zero skills.

*What do I do?* he asked himself. *Do I drain the wound? Do I just let it be? Why is she bleeding inside? Is there a fragment of the bullet causing it?* All these questions ran through his mind without an answer for any of them. Once again he felt helpless, powerless to do anything.

"Hope, you have to go save Hope," Charlotte said, grabbing his arm.

Her touch brought him back. "I'll go find her, but we need to take care of you first."

"Go find her."

Realizing that if she died, he'd have no way of knowing where Hope was, he thought to ask, "Where is Hope? Where do I find her?"

## HOPE

"Diary, my diary."

"Where is that?"

"Backpack," she replied.

Neal remembered the backpack she had been wearing. It was still on the ground at the other campsite. He raced over, grabbed it, and came back. He opened it, looked inside, and there it was, pink, fluffy and bedazzled.

"Hope, go."

"I will, I will," he said, thumbing through. "Where, did you write it down somewhere?"

"Yes."

He thumbed until the last entry and came upon a hand-drawn map with an address. Below it was the number of men who occupied the compound.

"Found it," he said.

"Go."

"No, I won't leave you."

"I can't make it."

She might be right, he thought. Right now he was batting zero for helping sick or wounded people. There were only a few things he was good at, and this wasn't one of them.

"Hope."

"Antibiotics, I have some. In my trailer, in the small kit, I have some antibiotics. That will help," he rambled as he ran to the trailer. "This will help, it has to."

"Hope, please."

"Found them," he said, pulling a bottle of amoxicillin from a small bag. He popped the lid, but his shaking hands caused him to drop a few onto the ground. "Damn it," he cursed. He went to her side and said, "Take this. It will help."

Charlotte didn't reply. She mumbled something unintelligible.

"Open up. Take the medicine."

She opened her mouth slightly.

He placed the capsule on her tongue and brought a bottle of water to her lips. "Here's some water. Swallow the pill."

She took a small sip but coughed the amoxicillin onto the ground.

"Work with me," he stressed. He picked another capsule from the bottle and placed it on her tongue. Lifting her head to make it easier to swallow, he again placed the bottle to her lips.

She sipped more, and this time was able to get the capsule down.

Feeling helpless and scared for her, he decided he was going to do the one thing he had power over. He would load her up in the trailer and set out to find Hope. He might lose Charlotte, but he was going to find her sister and make things right.

## Outside of Boulevard, CA

Neal stepped off the bike. Sweat poured off his face and even down his arms. He was drenched. The ride up the mountain was tough. Given he was still not a hundred percent, it made an already difficult ride more so.

This was where mindset came into play. Neal knew his weaknesses, but he also was aware of his strengths, and being someone who had the capacity to push himself beyond the limit, he was always one who could do so when everything counted on it.

He had lost so much and felt responsible for those losses. Now he had a small opportunity to redeem something, and the girls provided that.

Another dawn was coming and with it a variety of choices and situations. He checked on Charlotte, who was sleeping. Her fever was still raging, and the wound wasn't any better.

Before he left Ocotillo, he had calculated the distance to Hope's location to be a little under fifty miles, but it wasn't going to be an easy fifty, especially on a bike that was overloaded and operated by a person who had just survived botulism.

He pulled an old road map from his pocket and unfolded it. A road sign a quarter mile back read Boulevard. Using the key on the bottom, he estimated he'd ridden twenty-five miles. By the way he felt, especially his thighs and butt, he would have sworn he'd ridden a hundred.

With twenty-five miles down, he was halfway there, and fortunately for him he knew the remaining miles wouldn't be as hard as the last.

Happy with his results, he tucked the map back in his pocket, took a swig of water and looked for a safe place to rest. He knew getting to Hope as soon as possible was critical, but he had to get a few hours of rest. He was even willing to ride during the day, but not until he had given himself a much-needed break.

Just off the road on his right he saw a dry creek bed. It was far enough off the road and looked deep enough to provide the cover they needed.

Charlotte moved but didn't wake.

The distinct sound of car engines could be heard in the distance.

He paused to listen intently.

The sound was drawing closer but still far away. He was able to pinpoint that it was coming from the west.

He pushed the bike off the road, but as soon as he hit the dirt, the soft ground made it very difficult because of the weight of the bike and trailer.

The roar of vehicles grew louder.

He looked west. The highway rose gently and disappeared to the right behind a sloping hill.

He had time, but if he was going to hide, he had to move fast.

"Move!" he grunted as he pushed the bike another two feet. Seeing the futility of moving the bike with Charlotte in it, he scooped her up and walked to the dry creek bed.

Out of the corner of his eye, he caught a glimpse of something on the highway.

He looked and saw a large vehicle, but fortunately for him they were still a good half mile away. Using all his strength, he raced to the creek bed and slid down the embankment. When he hit the rocky bottom, Charlotte let out a groan. It wasn't enough to wake her, which was telling in and of itself.

He set her down and peeked back over the edge.

The hum was very loud now.

There wasn't just one vehicle; there were dozens by his rough count and all military-type MRAPs.

Always cautious, he kept his head down and watched as they zoomed by.

One by one they passed. He counted as they went. When the last one went by, his count was thirty-three.

*Where are they going?* he thought. He hadn't seen a convoy like that since shortly after everything collapsed. *Did they have anything to do with the warning he'd been given?* Whatever was happening, they were headed somewhere and fast.

With the emergency out of the way, he turned his attention to Charlotte.

Her head was cocked to the side and lifeless.

Alarmed, he shook her and asked, "Charlotte, you still with me?"

She flittered her eyes and whispered, "Hope."

"It's Neal. I'm just checking on you."

"Hope, get Hope."

"We're going there now. Just need a break. Sorry if I roughed you up getting you over here. I heard those trucks and I got scared. You just don't know who's cruising down the road," he said in a conversational tone.

She nodded off.

There wasn't any doubt the vehicles were military or government. Maybe he should have stopped them and asked for help. Did he just make a mistake? Life was so confusing. He'd heard nothing really positive about the federal government's response, some even speculating they were harming those who went seeking help. It was better he hadn't stopped them; things could have turned ugly.

He rested his head back against the rocks and closed his eyes. He could feel sleep coming, so he sat up. "Gotta go get the bike and set up." He shook his head, but his body was weary. He leaned back again and convinced himself that he'd close his eyes for just a wink.

Neal woke when he heard guttural growls. To his left and right were coyotes. It wasn't uncommon to see coyotes in Southern California. They were everywhere and were often seen in residential neighborhoods; however, most sightings happened at night. It was midday and the sun was riding high in the sky.

He kicked some rocks, causing the coyotes to scatter.

They regrouped and walked back, some growling and others barking; a coyote had a unique bark and howl. Neal had heard them a lot growing up and knew their barks indicated they were closing in on prey.

He pulled out his Sig and pointed it at the closest coyote.

A coyote ran up behind him and nipped at his neck.

He stood up and hollered, "Back away, back off."

Again they scurried away a short distance and regrouped to come back.

Neal spun around three hundred and sixty degrees and counted seven coyotes.

Charlotte wasn't moving. She lay on the hard ground, her head slumped over.

Another coyote ran at him.

He turned and yelled at it.

The coyote retreated.

Neal knew what he had to do because they would keep coming until they figured out a way to get him and her. He faced the one he thought was the alpha, aimed, and squeezed a shot off. The round exploded from the muzzle and struck the coyote in the neck.

That coyote yelped, ran a few feet, and collapsed dead.

"C'mon, motherfuckers!" he yelled, taking aim on another and shooting. This shot missed, as the coyote moved just as he shot.

The two loud shots scared the others. They retreated further away but still hung around.

Neal could feel that his face was sunburned. It was stupid of him to think he could just take a short nap. Angry with himself, he holstered the pistol, scooped up Charlotte, and climbed out of the creek bed.

His bike and trailer were exactly where he'd left them that morning.

Charlotte's head bobbed up and down as he hurried towards his bike. She was still alive but barely.

He looked down at her abdomen and it was huge. The swelling was so severe her shirt didn't fit and exposed the lower part of her belly. There he saw the deep purple and black skin.

"Stay with me," he said.

He reached the trailer and put her in carefully.

Barking behind him made him jump. He turned to see two coyotes had closed in. Pissed off, he unslung his rifle, took aim and squeezed off a round. The 5.56 round smashed into the coyote's head.

It dropped where it stood, dead before it hit the ground.

The second scurried away.

However, Neal had had enough; he took aim and squeezed off another round. This shot hit the coyote in the rear.

The coyote yelped and limped away.

Neal wasn't through. He kept his sights on it and shot several more times, hitting twice and missing once. Both rounds proved fatal as the coyote fell down dead.

The remaining coyotes kept their distance, some even running further away.

Feeling safe, he slung his rifle and pushed the bike back on the road. "Time to get out of here."

He had twenty-five miles to go, and if he rode hard, he'd be there before midnight.

## One Mile East of Golden Acorn Casino, Campo, CA

The signs on the road that told travelers of food and drink at the Golden Acorn Casino now informed them they were closing in on a federal camp.

In the rush to flee the coyotes and get the trip over as quickly as possible because of Charlotte's condition, Neal had forgotten about Bob's warning and had come close to entering the secured access lanes that led to the camp.

Before he blundered, he was able to get off the interstate and down to Live Oak Trail, a road that cut south and hopefully bypassed the federal camp.

The sun was closing in on the horizon, and soon the cover of darkness would help him. Until then he decided to pull off and rest behind a grove of trees twenty feet off the small road.

Immediately he checked on Charlotte, and her condition could only be described as critical. He tried to give her more antibiotics, but he couldn't get her conscious enough to take them. Nor would she drink any water. She was close to death, and once again he was proving to be incapable of keeping anyone alive.

A westerly breeze swept down and brought with it a putrid smell. The canvas cover of the trailer had small ash-like particles sprinkled on it. He brushed them away and thought nothing of them.

He started to reconsider taking her to the feds

and dropping her off. Maybe the stories weren't true. He was sure most rumors held some truth but also falsehoods. The issue was how more true were they than false.

A stiffer wind came and again the smell, but this time he noticed what could only be described as particulates drifting down out of the sky like snow. He held out his hand and caught a few. Some were dark gray while others were off-white.

He smelled them, but the individual pieces didn't hold an odor, but clearly there was something off in the air. The smell was something like a cross between burnt pork, plastics and diesel fuel. It was an odd smell, something he'd never encountered before.

Curious, he stepped away from the trailer until he found a small game trail and headed up it as it climbed up and gave him a vantage point of the surrounding area. Directly west he could see the casino, and the massive tent city that surrounded it was new and was the FEMA camp. To the south of the main casino building, five large pillars of black smoke rose; these had to be the source of the smell and ash. He gazed through his binoculars but couldn't get a good view of what was smoldering. He looked around the camp and didn't see anyone. The mix of white and olive green tents dotted the landscape to the east and south of the main casino building, with a multilayered chain-link fence topped with concertina wire running the perimeter. Large wooden towers stood at each corner, but no one manned them. He turned his attention to the highway and the fortified entrance. Again he saw no movement. It was odd, but maybe explained who he saw racing east earlier. The base also made sense as to why few cars were ever seen coming from the west. Many who attempted to go east ran into the camp, and he could only guess never made it out.

*Where is everyone?* he asked himself. That tent city looked as if it could house thousands, but those vehicles he saw going east weren't buses or anything large enough to carry thousands away. Did they come from there? Maybe they didn't, but whatever was happening at the camp had recently occurred.

Neal made his way back to the bike and found Charlotte half awake.

"How ya doing?" he asked, knowing it was a stupid question.

"I need to see Hope," she replied.

"We're close, I'd say less than twenty miles, but then I have a steeper challenge getting her," he said, stating the obvious.

"Hurry."

"I thought we had a bit of an obstacle due west, but it appears I was wrong," he said, referring to the camp.

"Hurry."

"Hurrying," he said, pushing the bike back onto the road and pedaling south.

When he reached the small unincorporated area of Live Oak Springs, he found it abandoned. Spray-painted marks on the doors told him the feds had come through and removed everyone. The town must have been emptied months ago, as tall grasses had already begun the slow battle of taking back the streets, and Mother Nature was encroaching on the homes and commercial spaces. Arriving at the intersection of Old Highway 80, he paused. Should he go right? That would take him into the camp. Or should he go left and try to find a way around it? By the looks of what he saw, the camp appeared to be empty, abandoned like the town behind him. Knowing time was not on Hope's side nor Charlotte's, he decided to risk it and go right. He pedaled along the narrow road until he came to the beginnings of the camp's south entrance. Interlocking Jersey barriers channeled him into a lane, which he slowly navigated until he came to the fortified gate, which lay wide open. The guard station was empty, and beyond he saw the thick smoke columns rising.

He continued, and the closer he got with each pedal made him feel more uneasy than the one before. Maybe it was a combination of the hastily abandoned camp, the smell, the smoke and the dying sun to the west casting long shadows his way. Whatever it was, something just didn't feel right.

Charlotte mumbled behind him, but she wasn't lucid anymore. When he did understand her, she was only repeating Hope's name over and over.

The air was now thick with the charred smell of something awful.

He was drawing closer. The light of the sun was still viable, so he'd be able to see without the aid of a flashlight what was smoldering. He could now make out that the five smoldering areas were massive ditches, and the bulldozers and other pieces of heavy equipment that had dug them were close by, but he still couldn't see what was lying in the bottom of the pits.

The sound of metal grinding and clanging came from below him. He looked down and saw brass ammunition casings and links covering the ground. There were literally thousands everywhere.

He stopped suddenly. A sick feeling came over him as he had his suspicions of what might have happened. The evidence was right there in front of him, but could it be real? He stepped off the bike. He wanted to see what was in the pits, but an apprehension overcame him. Did he need to know? Was this all in his head? If it was, what did it mean?

His stomach tightened. He just needed to press forward, away from the pits, out the far gate, and continue on. He wouldn't look, he couldn't. He got back on the bike and pedaled hard.

The smell washed over him again. It was strong and overpowering and made him nauseous. It was now a familiar smell; he knew it well.

*Should I stop and go see?* he thought. *No, keep pedaling.*

He was almost clear of the last pit when he braked hard. His curiosity was too strong; he needed to know. He briskly walked to the smoldering pit and looked down. When his eyes gazed upon the horror below, he turned and threw up. Using his sleeve, he wiped his mouth and again looked.

Below him, stacked feet high like cords of firewood, were the charred remains of people, thousands of them burned and unrecognizable.

Neal felt the urge to throw up again but held it back.

The rumors were true, all true. Those who went seeking shelter and comfort from the government found none, but why had they done this? What reason could anyone give? Was there some sort of viral outbreak? Or was this just murder? Memories of a TV show on The History Channel or some other network flashed through his mind. It was of the Nazis marching people into ditches and shooting them; then another of the crematoriums at places like Auschwitz with the black smoke rising from the stacks.

    Neal had seen enough. He raced back to the bike and rode off.

## CHAPTER SEVENTEEN

"Hope is like the sun, which, as we journey toward it, casts the shadow of our burden behind us." – Samuel Smiles

### Descanso, CA

The green glow from Neal's Casio G-Shock always comforted him. It reminded him of a different time; maybe it was because he'd had the watch for almost twenty years or that out of so much around him, it was one of the few reliable things he had left. Whatever the reason, the watch told him it was just a few minutes past three in the morning, and he had made it to the first stop, Charlotte's house.

She hadn't asked him to go there, nor had she told him where it was, but her diary was a treasure trove of information, one being her address.

To his surprise, she was still alive but wouldn't be for long, he feared. He carried her inside. The house was two stories, so he imagined her bedroom was on the second floor. He raced up and into the first bedroom he found. He gently laid her down on the thick pink duvet cover and smiled when he saw her name in big block letters above the bed. *What luck,* he thought.

He removed his headlamp and pointed it

towards the ceiling. The white light lit the entire room and provided a warm ambience. Tenderly he lifted her shirt and frowned when he saw her wound.

The stitches had popped out, and thick blood mixed with pus was oozing out heavily.

She was going to bleed out.

He couldn't believe she had made it this long. Was she holding on for Hope?

"Charlotte, I'm going to go get Hope now. I'm not sure when I'm going to return, but I'll come for you as soon as I can," he said, holding her hand.

She didn't move or acknowledge him, but she was alive, barely.

Seeing her reminded him of Beth. He kissed her hand and said, "I'll be back. You hang in there." He rushed out of the room and down the stairs and out the door. His adrenaline was pumping; he knew the next act in the Saving Hope play was going to be tough. Wanting to lighten the load, he emptied everything out of the trailer onto the ground. He quickly inspected his vest, ensuring his magazines were all there, before jumping back on the bike.

As he rode down the driveway towards uncertainty, he chuckled that Hope's savior wasn't coming on a white stallion but a Kona Dawg Deluxe mountain bike. He laughed even harder as he thought, *hi ho, Kona Dawg, away!*

## Guatay, CA

Using the cover of night, Neal navigated up the hillside, the same one that Bob had gone down when he fled the compound.

The concealment the night provided also put him at a disadvantage because he couldn't see where any guards were.

His plan was to move slowly from one covered spot to another, each time taking a moment to listen.

When he stopped each time, he took notice of how eerily quiet it was.

A glow of lights came from the far end of the compound. That had to be where the main house was according to the map Charlotte had drawn and he had committed to memory.

Neal remembered reading Charlotte's diary about the compound having generators, hence the lights.

He moved again and took up cover behind a jutting rock. He was thirty or so feet from the fence now. Again he listened for any movement or voices.

Nothing.

It was odd. He had been slowly advancing up the hill for an hour, and he hadn't heard one thing or seen a guard.

Between him and the fence, there didn't appear to be any cover. This was where he'd have to make a beeline, cut his way through, and enter the compound. From the fence his plan was to head straight up the hill and take cover behind the row of metal buildings. The center building was where Charlotte claimed to have been held and most likely was where Hope would be found if she was still there.

His preparation for the raid was thorough. He had six fully loaded thirty-round magazines for his rifle, four fully loaded magazines for his Sig, two knives and, more importantly, the will to see it until its end even if that meant his demise.

Neal readied himself, counted to three, and raced to the fence. When he got there, he pulled out his Leatherman tool, opened the wire cutters, and began clipping the individual links that held the chain-link fence to the pole. Four cuts later he was inside and running to the rear of the metal outbuildings.

He reached the first building, squatted down and again listened.

Nothing but quiet.

"What the hell? Where is everyone?" he said under his breath.

With no one around or in earshot, he stood and ran down the alley to the back door of the center building. He gulped, nervous that at any moment he'd encounter someone, and checked the knob by turning it slowly. Finding it was unlocked, he opened the door and peeked into the dark hall.

No one was there or at least not that he could see.

A light emanated from a single room on the left-hand side.

He stepped inside and with special care diligently took each step. He paused to listen, but still the place had an eerie silence to it. He lifted his right foot and extended it but felt something beneath it. He squatted down and felt with his available hand.

It was a body.

He stood and waited before again stepping forward and over the body. He reached the point in the hall where it teed off to a short hall that accessed the front entrance. The door at the end was open, and he could see a couple floodlights shining down on the main yard.

Several unidentifiable large lumps or piles lay outside the main house. He had a hunch what they were but needed his binoculars to properly identify them.

He retrieved them from a pocket on his tactical vest, looked through and focused. When the lenses cleared, he discovered the large lumps were bodies. *Interesting*, he said to himself.

Seeing more dead people began to fill him with confidence that he'd not find any opposition, but it also filled him with fear that Hope might be dead and his long journey there was for naught.

He pocketed the binoculars and proceeded to the door described by Charlotte. It was also the room where a faint light could be seen from under the door.

He reached out, touched the knob, and turned it to find it unlocked.

This was it, opening this door would signal the end to the short adventure. He slowly turned the knob until he heard the latch release. Unsure what he'd find on the other side, he raised his pistol and readied for a fight. In one swift movement he swung the door open and stood there.

He found the light originated from a small lantern in the center of the room. To the right he saw a bunk with no one in it, and on the left was another bunk, and there he saw a little girl.

Neal came in and asked, "Are you Hope?"

His abrupt entrance had scared her. She sat cowering with her legs drawn up to her chest and her face buried.

He stepped further inside the room and again asked, "Are you Hope?"

"Yes," she whimpered.

"I'm Neal. Your sister, Charlotte, sent me to rescue you."

Hope looked up, her face filled with joy upon hearing Charlotte's name and knowing she was being rescued.

# HOPE

He walked over to her, knelt down and asked, "Are you okay? Are you hurt at all?"

"No."

"Where is everyone?"

"Dead, everyone is dead," Hope answered.

"How?"

"Some poisoned, others killed each other, and a few left and brought back other bad men, who killed everyone else," Hope said. The poisoning harkened back to Bob's covert plan for revenge against Tony and his men.

"You're alone, no one else is here?" he asked.

"I'm alone."

"And you're unharmed?" he again asked, needing to make sure she didn't need attention.

"I'm fine. I hid from them. Things got really bad, so I went and hid."

"Thank God," Neal said, breathing a sigh of relief.

Hope looked past him and asked, "Where's Charlotte?"

"She's not well," Neal said, offering his hand.

"Where is she?"

Neal didn't want to be honest with her just yet; he needed her to remain calm so as to get her out of there with ease.

"Is she coming?" Hope asked.

"She's at home, your home. We need to get out

of here," he said and offered his hand.

She looked at it, hesitated, but felt he was a good man, so she took it.

He picked her up.

"No, Cuddles, grab Cuddles," Hope squealed, fearing her teddy bear would be left behind.

Neal looked on the bunk and saw the stuffed animal. He picked it up and handed it to her.

Hope warmly embraced Cuddles.

Not wasting any more time, he carried her out the back and towards the fence line.

"You're taking me home?" she asked.

"Yes."

They reached the fence line, and Neal put her down. "It's a very long walk, so are you sure you're okay?"

"Why not drive?" she asked.

"I wish. I don't have a vehicle."

"I know where there's a car," Hope said.

"You do?"

"Yes, it's back there," she said and pointed back to the compound.

He raised his eyebrows, curious. He then questioned why he didn't think of looking for one.

"Come on," she said and took his hand and led him back to the top of the hill. She pointed to a large shed to the right of the main house. "It's over there. I hid in there when everything went bad."

"Does it start?" he asked.

She shrugged her shoulders. "I don't know. I just know there's a car in there."

"Worth a try," he said then picked her up without asking and jogged across the yard.

The door to the shed was wide open. He turned on his headlamp, and right there in front of him sat the Dodge. He put her down, got behind the wheel and first thing checked if the keys were in the ignition already. They weren't, so he began to look. He popped the glove box and found nothing. He pulled down the visors, hoping they'd drop, but they weren't there either.

"If I were a key, where would I be?" he asked out loud.

Hope leaned in and pointed. "They're in there."

"Here?" he asked, pointing to the ashtray.

"Yes."

He pulled it out to find a set of keys attached to a rabbit's foot.

"I guess this does mean good luck," he said, taking the keys and inserting them in the ignition. Nervous, he looked at her and said, "Pray this starts."

She closed her eyes.

He followed suit by pressing his eyes closed and saying a short prayer. When he finished, he turned the key. The car roared to life. "Get in," he ordered.

Hope climbed over him and sat in the passenger

seat.

Being a parent, he looked at her and said, "In the back, get in the back. I'd say buckle up, but these old cars don't tend to have seat belts."

Hope did as he said.

The last thing stopping him from leaving was the garage door. He got out, pushed it up, and got right back into the car. He looked over his shoulder at Hope, who sat calmly with her hands folded on her lap, and said, "Let's take you home."

## Descanso, CA

Finally things were looking up and working out for Neal. He'd walked into the compound unopposed, found Hope alive, and the bonus was finding an operational car. However, his past experiences, mainly the most recent ones, told him that the string of good fortune would soon end.

Hope remained quiet the entire drive to her house.

He asked her questions, but by her one-word answers, he could tell she didn't have a desire to talk. Who could blame her; she was six years old and had been through something traumatic.

When Hope saw her house, she grew excited and antsy. She scooted close to the back door and waited patiently for them to pull up front.

Neal slowed as he approached the pile of supplies he had left in the driveway.

Hope opened the door and jumped out.

"Whoa, be careful. We're not stopped," Neal said.

Hope sprinted from the car and into the house. "Charlotte, Charlotte, I'm home, I'm home!" she shouted with joy. It was dark, but Hope knew every inch of her house.

Neal suddenly realized Hope might find Charlotte dead, and that would be a horrible discovery. With urgency he followed after her. He cleared the steps on the porch but tripped going into the house. He hit the floor hard and lay there for a second.

Upstairs, he heard Hope talking.

"Hope, I'm coming up," Neal said, getting to his feet and climbing the steps.

The light from the headlamp he had left behind cast its glow into the hall.

Neal approached the doorway but stopped short of walking in.

Charlotte was alive. She was lying still except for her right hand, which was petting Hope's hair.

Hope lay next to Charlotte, her head buried in her shoulder and her arms tight against her sides.

Neal could tell by Charlotte's blood-soaked shirt and pants that the bleeding was getting worse.

Feeling uncomfortable, he backed away from the door.

"No," Charlotte said, her voice just above a whisper.

He looked in and asked, "Are you talking to me?"

"Come," she said.

Feeling uneasy about encroaching on their intimate moment, he said, "It's fine. I was just checking on you."

"Please," Charlotte insisted.

Reluctantly he entered the room and stood only a couple feet in.

"Closer," Charlotte beckoned.

Hope watched Neal carefully while whispering to Charlotte.

"You seem better," Neal said as he took a few more steps into the room.

"Thank you," Charlotte said.

"You're welcome. Hey, what do you know, I did something right," he said.

"I love you, Hope," Charlotte said, her voice struggling. "I'm sorry about what happened."

Hope only whimpered.

"I need you to go with this man. He'll keep you safe," Charlotte said to Hope then looked at Neal. "You'll do that, won't you?"

"Yes, of course," Neal replied.

# HOPE

"No, I'm staying here with you," Hope said.

"I'm dying," Charlotte said.

"No," Hope whimpered.

Neal's heartstrings were pulling hard as he watched the two girls talk.

"You can't die," Hope said.

"Go with Neal. He'll keep you safe."

Unsure exactly what he should say, he said, "I will, I promise. You and I are going to go far away, on a boat."

"I don't want to leave," Hope whined.

"It's not safe here anymore. It's not safe anywhere," Charlotte said then grunted in pain.

"No, no, please don't die," Hope cried.

"Can I get you anything?" Neal asked.

"No," Charlotte replied. She closed her eyes. Tears streamed from the sides of her closed eyelids.

"Please don't leave me," Hope cried.

"Mom, is that you?" Charlotte asked, her eyes still shut.

Hope looked up at Charlotte.

"I've missed you," Charlotte said.

Hope began to sob.

Neal couldn't fight his own tears and let them stream unhindered down his face. In the span of a week he was witnessing another person leave this mortal existence.

"Dad, I hid like you told me," Charlotte said,

then unexpectedly opened her eyes.

Hope cried out, "Charlotte?"

Charlotte looked at Hope and said, "Mom says…"

A long pause followed.

"Be strong. Don't be sad…"

Another pause.

"Remember…live…" Charlotte said then gasped.

"Charlotte, no, please come back," Hope cried.

Neal too was overwhelmed with grief and began to sob. Watching Charlotte die brought back the memory of losing Beth and Karen.

The two cried and grieved. Both of them letting out the pain of loss so different but so similar.

Neal looked at Hope. He now knew his finding her wasn't random chance; something greater than him had enabled her to survive and given him the power to find her. This wasn't luck, this was a destined encounter.

Neal buried Charlotte alongside the grave where Drew had buried the girl's father. This was unknown to Charlotte, as Drew wanted to take her there to show he cared. However, fate never allowed that to happen.

Hope stood at the foot of the graves with a handful of wildflowers. Her tears were gone. She watched stoically as Neal placed the wooden crosses at the head of the graves. In her other arm, Cuddles, with his ever-present stitched grin, was tucked facing out.

Neal wiped his hands on his pants and took a place next to Hope. "Do you want to say anything?" he asked.

"I'll miss you, I love you," Hope said and put the flowers down.

"May they rest in peace," Neal said.

Hope turned around and walked towards the house.

Neal caught up to her and asked, "Are you okay?"

"I'm better now," she said.

"Good, I guess now is a good time to talk about where we're going."

Hope took a seat on the back steps and looked towards the rolling hills to the east.

He sat next to her and asked, "Ever been to Costa Rica?"

She shook her head.

"That's where we're going. It's nice there, I've been twice. My wife and I honeymooned there the first time, then went two summers ago with Beth, my daughter."

"You had a daughter?" Hope asked.

"Yes, she was pretty and sweet like you."

"Did she die?"

"Yes."

"I'm sorry."

"Me too."

"Tell me about Costa Rica?"

"Well, it's warm there all the time, and the water, the ocean temperature is perfect. You can go swimming without freezing your butt off. It's not cold like the ocean here. And the beaches, they're divine, they stretch for miles. The sand is silky soft and white. Oh, and the food, it's so good," he described as he motioned with his hands.

"Sounds nice."

"It is."

"Is it safe?"

He wasn't really sure if it was because he didn't really know what was going on anywhere else in the world, but he assumed the problems they had been experiencing only occurred in the United States. "Yeah, it is."

"When do we leave?"

"Tomorrow, we leave tomorrow."

"Are we driving?"

"No, remember I mentioned we're taking a boat," he answered. He then prayed it was still there. "We'll set out first thing in the morning and take mainly back roads and surface streets into and around the city."

She looked up at him and said, "Are you going to be my daddy now?"

"Um, well, I, um, that's a big word, as daddies are very special people. I don't think I've earned that title with you yet. But if you're asking me that hoping it means I'll be around to protect you, then the answer is yes, I'm here to stay. I'll make sure no harm comes to you."

Hope put Cuddles in his lap.

"What's his name again?"

"Cuddles, I think he likes you."

"Oh, does he? Well, I like Cuddles too," Neal said playfully.

"Tell me more about Costa Rica," Hope said.

"Do you want to know everything?"

"Tell me everything, it makes me happy," Hope answered.

Neal detailed all he knew about Costa Rica. From the food, places to stay, recreation, weather and people, he told her everything he could remember about it.

Hope set her head on his lap and listened, a smile creasing her chubby cherub like cheeks.

The more she smiled, the more he wanted to keep her smiling. He began to tell her stories of his trips there and all the things he'd done before. He promised to do those things with her too.

The late morning turned to the afternoon and

the two still sat and talked.

When the evening came, Neal prepared her dinner, and after they loaded the car together. Right from the start they worked like a team.

Later when he tucked her in, she asked, "Are there monkeys in Costa Rica?"

This single question initiated another diatribe about the country and the known wildlife.

Again she smiled, her green eyes twinkling as he described in great detail all he knew.

Later, when Neal closed his eyes, he thought about all that had happened. He missed Karen and Beth, but having Hope filled him with joy and gave him promise and faith. He just needed to make sure they made it to the harbor and that the boat was still there.

## CHAPTER EIGHTEEN

"We have always held to the hope, the belief, the conviction that there is a better life, a better world, beyond the horizon." – Franklin D. Roosevelt

San Diego Harbor

When Neal pulled into the parking lot of the marina, he sighed and celebrated internally for accomplishing the first and what could have been a disastrous leg of their journey.

Hope peeked through the grimy window and looked around. "Whoa, look at all the boats."

"We made it, thank God," Neal said.

"Which one is yours?" Hope asked.

"I'll show you," Neal said. He grimaced when he exited the car; his knees were sore from the long brutal bike ride. He suspected he had developed tendonitis only because he had suffered from it before.

Seeing the difficulty he was having, Hope hurried over and offered her hand.

Neal paused. He looked at her small hand and smiled. He shifted his gaze and looked into her green eyes. The loneliness was still present, but something had shifted. He could see a glimmer of something more, better. He laid his hand in hers and slowly stood. "Thank you."

She cracked a brief grin and pulled her gaze away from his.

The salty smell of sea air hit him. He cocked his head and looked out towards the marina.

Several seagulls reeled overhead and squawked their raucous calls.

He and Hope watched as they cruised past them and landed on a large pylon.

Neal couldn't help but think that the birds were going about their lives as if nothing had happened. Their lives were the same, well, maybe a bit different; gone was the easily available garbage left by humans, but for the most part their lives weren't affected. For all the talk and philosophizing that humans were the advanced species, they didn't act that way when the lights went out. The thousands of years of evolution hadn't removed the brutal instinct to murder or conquer. Mankind with all its luxuries, fashion, style, and so-called civilization wasn't any different than a wild animal; in fact, it could be argued they were worse. The events that followed the EMP didn't have to be a total collapse. If people had worked together for the greater good and rebuilt, there wouldn't have been a collapse on an apocalyptic scale. But none of these musings mattered, and thinking about them was a waste of time.

"Ever been on a boat?" Neal asked.

Hope shook her head no.

"Consider today your lucky day," he said with a smile. "Please be there," he mumbled under his breath. He limped past the rear of the car and looked directly down the long pier. When he saw the white hull and mast, he sighed.

Hope walked up to his side and asked, "Which one is yours?"

"It's that thirty-six-foot Beneteau, the big white one."

She cocked her head and shrugged her shoulders.

Feeling silly, he changed his response. "Oh, the big white sailboat at the very end, you see the mast and blue sail cover?"

Hope looked and nodded.

"Let's go check her out and see how's she's doing."

"She?"

"Yeah, boats are girls."

"They are?"

"Yeah."

"Why?"

"Good question, I don't really know why."

He took her hand and they walked together towards the pier.

"Tell me again about Costa Rica," she asked. Hearing the stories about their new home filled her with happiness and gave her hope for a better tomorrow. A joy emanated from her with the anticipation of hearing about their new home.

"It's a beautiful place, the beaches are filled with white silky sand, and the ocean water is warm, not like it is here."

"Is it safe there?"

He stopped and knelt down beside her. "No matter what, I'll keep you safe; I won't allow anything to ever happen to you. What I know is what happened here isn't happening down there."

"So it will be safe?"

He looked deep into her eyes and said, "It will be safe."

She lunged and wrapped her arms around him. "Thank you."

Her embrace brought tears to his eyes.

"Why are you crying? Are you sad?" she whispered.

"No, not at all, these are happy tears. Now let's get *Karen Knot* seaworthy."

"The boat's name is Karen Not?"

"Well, Karen for my wife and knot spelled with a k, representing speed at sea, kinda like miles per hour. It's a play on words; it means caring not or being not caring, make sense?"

Hope didn't quite understand nor cared; she smiled and hugged Cuddles.

He loved her smile. In fact, she seemed to smile

more than anyone he had ever known, and that said a lot. Beth had smiled often, but Hope clearly won the smile contest. "You have to be the happiest person I've ever known."

"I am?"

"Yeah, I've known quite a few people and you always seem to be smiling. How do you do it?"

"Do what?"

"Smile all the time."

"Is it bad?"

"Oh, gosh no, not at all, it's wonderful. You're wonderful. I wish I could smile more."

She again hugged him and said, "I'll help you do that."

He couldn't fight the tears; they again came to his eyes. "One day you'll give me your secret on being happy, deal?"

"I'll tell you now."

"Will you, please?"

"Mommy told me all the time that in order to be happy you have to let go of what makes you sad."

"Wow, so profound for a six-year-old."

"Mommy had us memorize it."

"How do you do it?"

"I told you."

"No, how are you able to let go of the things that make you sad?"

"The only things that have made me sad were

my family dying, but I know I'll see them again."

"You do?"

"Yes. I know they're in heaven and God is hugging them right now."

"He is?" Neal asked. He wasn't mocking her; he was genuinely curious. He had never been an overly religious person, and with everything that had occurred lately, he had lost more of his spirituality and questioned if God truly existed.

"I saw him; he told me they were fine."

"Hmm."

Hope looked at him and said, "You don't believe me."

"I didn't say that. I just haven't met anyone who's talked to God."

"Can we go now?"

"Um, sure, but I hope you don't mind if I ask more questions later. Is that okay?"

"Sure, it's fine."

They walked slowly down the pier. Silence washed over them as they drew closer to the boat. Neither really knew what lay ahead, but for Neal, the open sea offered a better life than what they were leaving.

Getting the *Karen Knot* seaworthy didn't take as long as Neal thought. Of course, it was harder having to do it all by himself, and it had been a while since he had been on her, but he quickly remembered the little things and in short order had her on the water.

Hope was beyond thrilled. The cool bay air felt good against her face. Giggling, she raised Cuddles high above her head and pretended the stuffed teddy bear was flying.

San Diego Bay was smooth sailing, but the ocean beyond would be entirely different.

Knowing a game would make it fun for her, he said, "Permission to man the helm, Captain?"

She looked at him funny.

"You're the captain and I'm the first mate. Now give me the order to take the helm."

"Take the helm."

"Or as a captain of a boat would say, *permission granted*," he said, lowering his voice to make him sound like an old salty sailor.

"Permission granted," Hope said. She then hugged Cuddles and asked, "What does Cuddles do?"

Neal got behind the wheel and looked towards Point Loma and the inlet that flowed from the Pacific into San Diego Bay. "We'll make him our security."

"Like a policeman?" Hope asked, walking up next to Neal.

"I was thinking a Marine or SEAL."

"A seal, um, I don't think seals can keep us safe,"

Hope replied, not understanding what Neal meant by the term SEAL.

"Then we'll make him a salty Marine, and his rank will be gunny. That's it, Gunny Cuddles," Neal joked.

"Yeah, Gunny Cuddles to the rescue." Hope cheered, holding the teddy bear high again above her head.

"Look up there," Neal said, pointing to the lighthouse above them on the right.

"What's that?" Hope asked.

"That's the Point Loma Lighthouse, and that over there to the left, or port side in sailing terms, is North Island Naval Center. So we'll exit out the inlet here, you see we're now heading due south; then we'll turn slightly and head out to deeper ocean."

"Where's the ocean?"

"You can see a bit right there, but the whole ocean is just on the other side of Point Loma. We can't really see it because of these tall cliffs."

Hope nodded and again held Cuddles high just when a brisk ocean wind came and swept Cuddles out of her grasp. "No!"

Cuddles fell onto the deck.

She bent over to get him but kicked him accidently. He skirted across the deck and stopped just shy of going overboard.

Neal quickly grabbed her for fear she'd fall over.

He reached out and picked up Cuddles. Holding Hope tight, he said, "You can't just run around on the deck here. You can fall over."

Scared, she simply replied, "Okay."

"Here's Cuddles."

"Gunny Cuddles," she reminded him.

Neal got behind the wheel and made a slight adjustment. They were now set to sail out of the inlet and into the ocean. "I need you to stay put right here. Just hold the wheel; make sure it doesn't move. I'm going below deck to get something."

"Okay."

"Don't move. Just stay right here."

"I'm scared."

"You'll be fine. I'm just going below to get you a life jacket. I'll be right back."

After that incident, Neal was nervous. Why he hadn't gotten her suited up with a life vest before was stupid on his part. He raced below deck to go find her one.

"Do you have one for Cuddles?" Hope asked.

Normally he would have just dismissed her or placated the question, but he wanted to make her happy. "You know, we just might have a very teeny tiny jacket that will fit him."

"Good, I want him to be safe; I don't think he knows how to swim."

Neal opened the cabinets the jackets were

normally stowed in but couldn't find them. "Argh," he grunted. He went from one cabinet to another. Unable to find them, he thought for a second, and then he remembered where they might be. He lifted up a cushioned bench seat in the dining space, and voila, there they were.

The ship began to rock more, indicating they were heading out to sea.

Neal grabbed several jackets. He then heard Hope speaking loudly.

"Hello, hi, hello," Hope said.

*She must be playing make-believe*, he thought. He stepped up the ladder well and onto the deck. He dropped the jackets in shock when he saw the towering gray hull of a massive warship.

Hope was right where he left her. She was waving to the sailors on board, who were waving back with big smiles on their faces.

Neal's jaw dropped. The beaming and smiling faces wore uniforms he hadn't seen before. These weren't American sailors; they were from somewhere else.

They sailed past the ship without incident.

Neal looked back and saw the bright red flag with the sickle and stars; it was the flag of the People's Republic of China.

"Look," Hope said and pointed north.

Neal snapped his head in that direction, and

what he saw along the coast as far as the eye could see was frightening, not because of the sheer size and number of ships but because of why they were there.

All the way to the horizon and stretching from the coast to the west out of sight was an armada of ships bigger than anything he'd ever seen in his life, hundreds by a rough count, maybe thousands depending on how far north they went. This wasn't a humanitarian force, this was an invading force.

"Are they coming to help?" Hope asked.

He took her hand and replied, "I don't think so."

"They're bad people?"

"Yes, I think they are."

"What's going to happen?"

"I don't know, but we left just in time," Neal said. With Hope in tow, he walked to the wheel and adjusted their course away from the ships. To the south, the ocean beckoned. He wasn't sure what lay out beyond the horizon, but the unknown seemed to offer greater certainty than what lay behind them.

The United States was gone with no promise of return.

Neal knew he couldn't make guarantees, but he would do anything and everything to keep his promise to Karen and Charlotte to ensure Hope would be able to live her life in relative safety.

They both had experienced tragedy and bitter loss, but together they could find something better. Together they could establish a new family. They'd left the country they had called home, but they weren't leaving home as much as they were…Going Home.

## THE END

HOPE

# READ AN EXCERPT FROM AN UPCOMING BOOK BY A. AMERICAN

## CRY HAVOC

After a campaign full of infighting and mudslinging, Hillary Clinton narrowly dodged being indicted. Or so we were led to believe. She went on to win the election for president of the United States in what appeared to be a landslide. As bad as this would become, it could have been worse. But there were serious issues with the election. Her victory was so overwhelming, in fact, that many believed it a farce. This caused even more problems; the campaign had already stirred up a lot of angst in the country. Her predecessor, Obama, ran a campaign that really played the social equity angle, some called it the race card. Either way you looked at it, a wedge the size of Mount Everest was driven through the country. There were cries of rigged elections from the right. The left shouted from every microphone they got in front of that this was the true season of change; after all, the nation had spoken, a second time. The people of America really did want the hope and change started by President Obama that was sure to continue under a historic Clinton presidency.

One of the first things the president did was to

push Congress and the Senate to ratify the Small Arms Treaty. Oh, there was great outrage from the reps on the right, lots of pulpit pounding and chest-thumping, but in the end it passed both chambers with a nearly ninety percent yes vote. This was gasoline on the fire. The second act of the president was to capitulate to Iran and acknowledge their right to self-defense and, in that light, their right to nuclear weapons. She legitimized their nuclear program with the stroke of a pen. This process was begun under Obama; Clinton just acknowledged it. Israel went mad; they pled their case in the public court. But with so much going on at home, many Americans simply ignored it or paid little attention.

Further emboldened, radicals in the Middle East pressed their campaigns of terror and fear throughout the world. Israel was under near constant attack from the West Bank. When ISIS was defeated despite the best efforts of the Obama and Clinton administrations, Iran was even further emboldened. Hezbollah began direct action operations against Israel. Of course, publicly they denied this. But with the full backing of the Russians, there was little the world could do short of a full-scale world war.

But contrary to what many would have believed, President Clinton wasn't a dove when it came to this, she was certainly an eagle. And while many praised her strong rhetoric towards Russia and

Iran as strong and patriotic, they had no idea what was to come was already a foregone conclusion. She was only playing her part. And this wasn't another war on terror or for land or even oil. This was a war over the financial control of the world. The world was changing. The dollar was dying, and there was only one way to save it.

The trail to destruction was thus begun. Oh, there were other potholes along the way, but these events were to have such a profound effect on the country that it would be forever changed. When Obama knelt at the feet of the Persians, figuratively if not literally, it emboldened the Iranian leadership. When the president proposed a further reduction in nuclear arsenals with the Russians, the government of Putin eagerly agreed. A great victory in the name of humanity was made out of the decommissioning of upwards of sixty percent of the US arsenal. The Russians played up the plan in the media; appearances between the two leaders were plastered all over the MSM. The Russians, however, were not decommissioning anything.

Under the Small Arms Treaty, it was announced to the nations of the world that the private ownership of military-grade weapons was now outlawed. Much was made that America, reputed to be the last superpower, had the greatest number of such weapons in private hands. The fact that the US administration ratified the treaty, then went even further by reducing its nuclear arsenal, heralded a new era in global peace while at the same time continuing to bang the drums of war. The rest of the world might have bought this, but the owners of the more than three hundred million guns in the US certainly didn't. And yet, here, another wedge was driven into the nation.

There were many gun owners in the country that certainly believed military-grade hardware should be outlawed. They joined the applause of the Treaty. Those that believed that high-capacity magazines should be outlawed joined the orgy of praise as well. That was until it was revealed that additional wording was added that banned any weapon that was capable of mechanical self-loading. In the beginning this caused some confusion and misconceptions. When it was revealed that any magazine-fed weapon, regardless of capacity, was banned, the cries of violating the Constitution grew louder. When it was further revealed that the term *magazine* also included tube-fed weapons, the cries reached a crescendo. Now there was no doubt what the intentions behind this Treaty were, the virtual total disarmament of the American people.

The events happening around the globe faded from the minds of most Americans, who were so caught up in their fading freedoms that they paid less and less attention to the happenings on the global scale. And while they wouldn't pay attention for now, a time was fast approaching when they would no longer be able to ignore it.

For many in the prepper community, the writing was on the wall. All across the country people were making decisions. Some were headed to their BOLs, others were trying to buy up whatever ammo was left out there, and prices were astronomical. There would be no more shipments, no more mags, no more parts, nothing. All those people that figured they would see "it" coming and head out and use their credit cards to prepare were caught with their pants down, and Big Brother was squeezing Astro Glide into his hand.

When the TSA started to set up roadblocks and search vehicles, the shit hit the fan. The feds decided to go big. Many people were caught off guard by the TSA being the ones to man these roadblocks. But the ice had already been broken on that issue years ago. Of course, it was called training for terror operations back then. The feds just didn't mention who those terrorists would be: we, the people.

The first roadblocks were set up in Michigan. It was bait, and the Michigan Militia took it. When the militia heard that the TSA goons were searching people on the interstates, confiscating and arresting people for possession of firearms, even though the "grace period" wasn't up, they made their move. A unit of the militia planned a quick op when they heard of a roadblock nearby.

Using six vehicles, they approached the roadblock from both directions. This particular roadblock was on a frontage road that paralleled Highway 96 outside of Lansing. The lead car had two militiamen in it. As they approached the roadblock, they were challenged by the TSA and asked if they had any weapons. When they replied they did, they were ordered from the car. Both of them were wearing body armor with plates front and back. Most of the attention of those manning the roadblock were focused on the two "noncompliant" passengers.

It was then that the other twenty-five members emerged from the other five SUVs and opened fire on the TSA, DHS and State Patrol officers at the roadblock. The incident would forever be referred to as the "Lansing Incident"; it would be a battle cry for the patriots of the nation and the anvil against which all freedom-loving men and women of the US would be hammered against. Four militiamen were killed as well as two troopers, two DHS personnel and four from the TSA. The firefight was intense and short, the result being that almost all the vehicles at the scene belonging to any of the agencies involved were burned through the use of homemade thermite grenades.

The militia managed to escape from the scene, recovering their fallen comrades. None of them were ever caught, although the MSM would report otherwise. This was our Concord; this was the spark that started it all. America was now a police state. And to make matters worse, America was also about to go to war.

This was the moment the administration had been waiting for. Before the fires were even out in Lansing, the attorney general was issuing decrees to local, state and federal law enforcement agencies. All weapons in private hands were to be seized. To get around any Constitutional or legal loopholes, the president enacted several executive orders, not the least of which was 13603; section 501 was to have a profound effect on the citizens of the nation. This particular section of the EO was headed by Employment of Personnel and allowed the establishment of the National Executive Defense Reserve or NEDR. It was created under the auspices of training civilians in executive level positions in the federal government. In reality it was a cover to create a private, federal police force, answerable only to the president and the attorney general.

KLB Inc was awarded an indefinite delivery contract to provide for detention and housing of "suspects and subversives", utilizing the guidelines established in the NDAA. The National Defense Authorization Act allowed for the indefinite detention of American citizens without any Constitutional protections. The Council of Governors was instructed to assist in the DHS with the activation of the Regional FEMA camps. These camps would be used to house persons arrested under provisions of the NDAA. Soon American citizens would be facing American troops on the streets of the nation. That was unless their attention was focused elsewhere.

Daniel Taylor lived in a four-story apartment building on Century Cir, off of I-85 in downtown Atlanta. He worked in the IT department of one of the banks in Atlanta and attended the University of Phoenix DeKalb Learning Center across the street from his apartment. In his position he was responsible for keeping the network secure from the constant, daily attacks on the bank's network. He was one of many who lived in cubicle land, staring into computer monitors all day. Once he finished his degree, he hoped to be promoted out of the gopher farm and upstairs, but for now, this was his life.

While cyberattacks on banks were nothing new, things were really getting bad lately. He and the others tasked with securing the bank's servers from attacks were only just able to keep up. And it wasn't just them. In white papers that circulated through the IT world, it was now openly acknowledged that the early stages of war were already in motion. Power plants, utility providers, banks, traffic networks, military and law enforcement networks across the nation were under constant and crippling attacks. While it wasn't stated publicly, those in the industry knew where the attacks were coming from.

Daniel's girlfriend, Christy, lived nearby in a different apartment. She had hinted several times at wanting to move in together, but so far he'd been successful in dodging that particular bullet. He wasn't ready for any sort of commitment. He liked his freedom, and from the talks around the water cooler and the employee lounge, married life came with way too damn many restrictions for him. He enjoyed his weekends in north Georgia, where he camped, hiked and fished. He liked his time in places like the Bowmans Island unit of the Chattahoochee River.

This was where he got away from the hustle and bustle of Atlanta. Up there it was quieter and there were fewer people. On the weekends he would load his Wrangler up and head out of town with his camping gear and a cooler, not to return until sometime Sunday afternoon. Sometimes Christy would go with him; she wasn't much of a camper, but was learning to like it. Watching the sun set from the top of a ridge or the sun rising over a secluded pond made it worth the trip. Most of the time, however, he was alone, and that was how he liked it.

All through the election, things in Atlanta got progressively worse, culminating in riots. The National Guard was brought in to put them down after the police were overwhelmed. This caused even more riots and problems. Two Guardsmen were shot and killed and their weapons stolen. The result was for the governor to authorize the Guard troops to shoot armed individuals and looters on sight. Seventeen people were killed, fourteen of them black; this just added fuel to the fire of racial inequality. The world was coming apart at the seams and the band played on.

Daniel let out an evil laugh as he jumped and slapped the sign that indicated the elevator. He packed into the first elevator that stopped on his floor. From the looks on the faces of the people already on it, they were not happy with one more person squeezing on. He simply smiled and edged his way in. When the doors opened in the lobby, he was the first one off and made a mad dash for the parking garage.

Traffic was a nightmare, as was typical for Atlanta. While he was ready to get home and load up, he wasn't letting it get to him. Where he was headed, there wouldn't be any traffic. The one thing he did notice was all the police on the road. On his ride home Daniel saw more Atlanta cops, state troopers and sheriff deputies than he ever had. Several times he saw these officers putting people in handcuffs and stuffing them in the back of their car. It seemed like the number of people being arrested was increasing.

Daniel flipped on the radio, looking for a distraction. He was scanning through the stations, looking for something to listen to that wouldn't drive him nuts. The radio stopped on one of the local talk stations; Rush Limbaugh was on. He was ranting and raving about how the Republicans had completely caved on Israel, how they were done, they would never be a viable party again. Well, this certainly wasn't helping his sanity, so he punched a key on the radio and smiled as Kid Rock's "Cocky" started.

His cell phone rang. Looking down, he saw Christy's name on the screen, and a smile came across his face.

He tapped the screen. "Hey, sexy." This was his standard answer.

"Hey, babe, where are you?"

"Stuck on 85, sitting in traffic. Where are you?"

"At my apartment. What do you want to do this weekend? I was kinda hoping we could go to Buckhead tonight; you know, take me out to do what I want and you can do what you want." Christy's voice trailed off into a breathy seductive tone.

Well now, that was an offer he had to think

about. "I was hoping to head up north and check out that trail we found the last time we were out." He didn't say anything more than that, not "do you wanna come?" or anything; he was going to have to see what sort of mood she was in.

"Aw, come on, baby, we haven't gone out in, like, forever. I wanna go out; take me out tonight, please," Christy cooed into the phone.

Daniel's hand fell into his lap. He looked up at the rag top of his Jeep, his mouth hanging open. In his mind he was screaming *why, why, why*, but he knew he couldn't say that to her. He hated to "go out"; barhopping, going to clubs and being dragged out onto the dance floor was simply not his thing. But he liked Christy, for a couple of reasons. That last thought brought him back around, and he put the phone back to his ear.

"Sure, babe, we can go out. I need to get home and get a shower and change. Just come over when you're ready," he finally said.

The conversation didn't last much longer than that. Christy was excited at the thought of spending the night in Buckhead; Daniel was just as miserable at the thought. Then he smiled, knowing the hours he would spend slogging through the bars and clubs would be worth it when they got back to his place.

He finally made it home and into his apartment on the second floor, closing the door with an audible sigh. His first order of business was to get out of the corporate monkey suit and into something more comfortable, so he headed for his bedroom and returned wearing a T-shirt and shorts, feeling far more relaxed. He knew Christy would be a couple—hell, more than a couple—hours before she showed up, and he grabbed a beer and turned on the TV. Fox News and CNN were running talking heads from opposite sides of the gun debates; MSNBC was interviewing some clown from the EU who was pontificating about the US's role in the global economy and how they weren't acting very responsibly.

None of this was doing anything to improve his mood, though, and he flipped to the guide and found *Jackass: The Movie*, which was exactly the sort of mind-numbing entertainment he wanted. Daniel decided to take a shower and start getting ready; turning up the volume on Johnny Knoxville's antics, he headed for the shower.

He was sitting on the couch, watching a piece about Rommel on the Military Channel when he heard that distinct knock on the door. He flipped off the TV and grabbed his keys and wallet before heading towards the door. Opening the door, he was greeted with an amazing sight, Christy had one arm resting on the door frame over her head. She was wearing what was often referred to as a little black dress, little being the key word, and she was smokin' hot in it. Adding in the black heels and the fact the small dress barely contained her chest, he questioned the plan of going out, thinking staying at his place would be better. But then, if he took her out and let her party it up, it would certainly pay off.

"Damn, you look fine," Daniel said as he stepped towards her.

Christy wrapped her arms around his neck and smiled, revealing her beautifully perfect white teeth; then she pushed herself up on her toes and leaned in and kissed him. "You don't look so bad yourself," she said with a smile, stepping back to check him out, "and all by yourself, I'm so proud."

Daniel did a little pirouette. "Not bad, huh?"

Christy reached out and grabbed his ass. "Not bad at all, so where we going?"

He had planned what he would say to this question. "I thought we would start at Churchill's." Before he even finished saying it, he started to smile, knowing how she felt about the British-style pub.

Christy spun and started to walk towards the stairs, tossing her little black purse over her shoulder. "I'll pretend I didn't hear that."

They started the night at Aria Restaurant off East Paces Ferry Road, a trendy, upscale little place with great food and prices that reflected it. Daniel knew this night was going to cost him, but since he wasn't going to the woods this weekend, he was going to make it as enjoyable as possible, and keeping Christy in bed all weekend would certainly be enjoyable.

They enjoyed their dinner; he had salmon, and Christy a chicken something or other. Because of the difference in dishes, they had two different bottles of wine at the table as well. Neither of them wanted dessert, and Daniel quickly paid the bill and they were off to find some music and people.

Daniel was pulling out of the parking lot when he asked Christy where she wanted to go. Her reply was no help. "Surprise me." All he could do was roll his eyes as he pulled out onto the road. This scenario had entered his mind, and having been a Boy Scout, he was ready and headed down Paces Ferry to Piedmont and made a right. The stars were lining up tonight, and a car was pulling out of a spot in front of the Havana Club as he pulled in.

Looking over at Christy, he asked, "Feel like dancing tonight?" His eyebrows jumped up and down as he did.

Christy was obviously surprised. Being a typical guy, he tried to avoid dancing at all costs, and for him to suggest it was certainly a surprise. "You mean you're actually going to dance with me tonight?"

Daniel looked over at her as he put the Jeep in park. The small silver chain she wore around her neck caught his eye; the little pendant rested in the top of her ample cleavage. He looked a little lower until the little black dress covered his desires. He reached across to her seat and laid his hand on her thigh, running it slightly up her leg under the dress. "You look amazing tonight. Wanna dance?"

Christy took a deep breath, her mouth slightly open, and began to vigorously nod her head. "Yeah, oh yeah, let's go."

Inside, the bar was packed with all the young and beautiful of Atlanta. Techno dance music filled the place, and bodies on the floor writhed to the rhythm. As soon as Christy broke the plane of the door, her arms went up and she began to shake her ass to the music. They spent the next several hours dancing and drinking. Christy was having a great time, and he knew he would later. It was the only thing that kept him going.

Daniel needed a break from the dance floor and told Christy he was going to get them a drink. She nodded and turned back to the writhing crowd. Daniel went to the bathroom to take a leak. Of course, there was an "attendant" in there, an older black man sitting on a stool. Daniel saw him when he came in and rolled his eyes. After finishing his business at the urinal, he went to the sink. The soap dispenser was gone, and the old man held out a bottle of liquid soap. Daniel stuck his hands out, and the old guy pumped a few squirts in his hand.

As he washed his hands, he looked over to the paper towel dispenser, and just as he suspected, it was empty. A smirk ran across his face. When he finished, the old man tossed him a hand towel and he dried his hands. Sitting on the counter was a small basket full of bills, he handed the towel back to the old guy and he tossed it into a basket on the floor. Now he was expected to tip this guy for some soap and a towel.

The old man was smiling at him. Daniel looked at him, patting his pockets. "Sorry, man, don't have any cash. I'm going to the bar for some drinks and I'll take care of you next time."

"Jus' don't forget about me," the old guy said with a wink.

Daniel left the restroom, shaking his head at the thought of having to pay to take a piss, and fought his way to the bar. He was trying to get the attention of one of the hot bartenders, which appeared impossible, and occupied his time with one of the huge TVs behind the bar. A local news anchor was on the screen; behind her was a line of riot police forming a skirmish line. Daniel was absentmindedly watching when the scroll at the bottom of the screen said, "Riot at Centennial Place."

He immediately left the bar, heading for the dance floor to find Christy. He found her dancing with some Latin guy with no shirt. He wedged in between them, and she threw her arms around his neck and kissed him.

Pulling away from her, he shouted over the music, "We gotta go!"

She was still smiling and dancing to the music. "What!" she shouted back.

"We gotta go!" he shouted again.

She simply smiled back at him, grabbing his hands and pulling him towards her. Daniel gripped her right hand and pulled her from the dance floor. She tried to protest, pulling away.

"What the hell?" Christy asked.

"Look, there's a riot starting over at Centennial Place. We need to get the hell outta here before they bring in the National Guard and start shooting people."

"Why? That's blocks from here. Come on, come back out and dance with me."

"No, I'm leaving. I'm not getting caught in that shit. You coming?" Daniel asked.

The tone of his voice or maybe his posture drove the point home. "Fine."

Daniel led her out of the club and to the Jeep. He was putting her in on the passenger side when she wrapped her arms around him again. Christy pulled him to her and started to kiss him, but the sounds of a police helicopter flying low overhead brought Daniel's attention back to more pressing matters, even if they weren't as enjoyable as what was happening.

Backing away from her, he said, "Hold that thought. Let's get out of here first."

She leaned back into her seat and smiled, closing her eyes. Daniel looked in the direction of Centennial Place at the glow rising above the buildings. Police sirens filled the air as well as police and news helicopters. All he wanted to do was get back to his apartment as fast as he could. By the time he got around the Jeep and into the driver's seat, Christy was passed out, her head slumped over on the door.

He pulled out of the parking lot and headed back towards the apartment. Traffic was building, and police were beginning to shut down intersections. Daniel was forced to take several turns he didn't want to, and as a result, he was getting farther and farther from his apartment.

What should have been a twenty-minute drive ended up taking over an hour and a half. Daniel never saw any trouble, he never got close enough to whatever was going on to see, and that was fine with him. Pulling into the parking garage, he managed to wake Christy up without too much trouble and helped her get to the elevator and into the apartment.

Once inside, Christy sat on the edge of his

bed and he went into the bathroom. For a moment he leaned on the sink, looking into the mirror. He'd wanted to get out of town this weekend, out into the woods, and he'd let her talk him into staying here, and now there was a frickin' riot. He quickly washed his face and kicked his shoes off, trying to relax.

Opening the door, he saw her lying naked on the bed, propped up on her elbows. The light from the bathroom lit her side facing him, and a smile spread across his face. Maybe staying here wasn't such a bad idea.

Daniel woke up when light streamed through the blinds in the morning. Shielding his eyes with his hand, he sat up, then went and closed them. Christy was lying there, sound asleep; she looked so good. Running a hand over her ass, he covered her with the sheet and headed for the kitchen. He needed his hangover remedy, not that he'd drunk that much, but the combination of the alcohol, the music and the stress of the ride home made him feel like he'd drunk an entire liquor store.

After taking two Excedrin and drinking a huge glass of water, Daniel went to the fridge and dug out some cream cheese. From a paper bag on the counter, he pulled out a huge everything bagel then looked inside and found a plain one. With his bagel fixed, he headed for the living room and dropped onto the couch, flipping on the TV.

He changed the channel to Fox News to see what was going on in the world. What he saw shocked him. On the screen was a view of Centennial Place. Cars were on fire as well as some buildings in the distance. It looked as though there were hundreds of police, but unlike last night, these were not riot cops. The shields and clubs were gone, replaced with armored vehicles and rifles.

The reporter on the scene was saying something about "an unknown number killed in the fighting". He sat up on the sofa, leaning forward. In the background of the shot, it appeared that a large section of the area was blocked off, and there were bodies visible in a couple of places. The reporter came back into view again, and he could see she was crouching behind the corner of a building as the cameraman leaned out to get shots of the action. Gunshots could be heard in the audio; the camera bounced and jerked with each report.

Daniel sat there shaking his head. *People are fucking nuts,* he thought to himself. Watching what was unfolding before him, he started to get a little nervous and got up, returning to the kitchen. He felt like he should be doing something, but what? The riot was still pretty far from his place and shouldn't be a problem, but better safe than sorry. Daniel went through the cabinets really quick to get an idea of what he had on hand. Being a bachelor, naturally they were quite bare. Deciding it would be a good idea to have a little more on hand, he figured a trip to the store wouldn't hurt.

Look for CRY HAVOC<br>June 2016

# READ AN EXCERPT FROM NEMESIS: INCEPTION BOOK ONE: THE NEMESIS TRILOGY BY G. MICHAEL HOPF

---

### February 22, 2015

*"The two most important days in your life are the day you are born and the day you find out why."* – Mark Twain

### Crescent, Oregon

*"Lexi...Lexi...WAKE UP!"* the reoccurring voice from her dreams shouted.

She sat up quickly, her heart racing as a cold sweat clung to her skin. She wiped the sweat with her shaking hands and blinked in an effort to clear her eyes, but it did no good in the pitch-black space. Fumbling, she found a glow stick, cracked it and shook vigorously. Soon a yellow glow lit the dark crevasses of the room. Her vision adjusted, but the room offered nothing for her champagne-colored eyes to feast upon. The walls were lined with boxes, and at her feet, a large metal shelf held cans and bottles. The smell of the room at first was off-putting, but she soon didn't notice the mix of dust, cardboard and stale beer. The damp back storeroom of The Mohawk Bar and Grill wasn't luxury accommodations, but having a relatively safe place to rest your head from the winter cold and dangers of the road came pretty close. At first she had refused the offer for shelter, only accepting it when she realized the place was full of provisions and an older single man who she sized up as beatable in a fight. After surviving for two months in the new world, her situational awareness was always on. She chalked it up as one of the primary reasons she was still alive.

Lexi rubbed her eyes and grunted in frustration when the nightly dream that prevented her from getting the rest she needed popped in her mind. She had grown weary from her inability to sleep soundly. Before the collapse, sleeping had been one of her best friends. Not a weekend morning went by where she'd be awake by eleven, and her weekday mornings were a struggle to rise, each morning a repeat of the last as she hit the snooze button a dozen times. Now her sleep, if one could call it that, was punctuated with night terrors and restlessness.

A knock at the door startled her. She reached under the pillow and grabbed her pistol, a Glock 17 9mm semiautomatic.

"Lexi? Are you all right? I heard you scream," the voice said from behind the door.

She looked and saw a dark shadow blocking the

dim light from underneath the door. She didn't know John, much less completely trust him. She had only met him a week before.

After her narrow escape from a small band of marauders, she had crashed the motorcycle she had stolen along the highway south of town. A small detachment of Marines had found her and offered assistance.

Not having a place to call home, the Marines took her to the Mohawk. The Marines had created a relationship with John not long after arriving in town. Crescent was a small town, and with no other business operating besides the Mohawk, it provided a place for what remained of the community to gather. John had no family and nothing else, so keeping his only love, the Mohawk, open was a natural decision for him. He quickly ran out of perishable foods, but his supply of alcohol was abundant and part of his plan was to use it as currency. John was a large burly man, his black hair now streaked with silver. His wife had left him years ago and, with no children, the townspeople were family.

During her stay, she had spent her time working out and training out back with her long sheath knives. Then she would find an excuse, any would do, to find adequate time to drink.

John found himself watching her and was impressed with her skills. In fact, he was curious who he had staying in his back room. Today he made it a point to find out.

"Lexi, you in there?" he asked again, this time trying the knob. The door was locked.

Lexi looked at the door; her instincts born out of the chaos of the new world told her not to open it. Not truly knowing John and with her numerous negative experiences, she remained hesitant to trust anyone. Then her reasonable and pragmatic side won out. She didn't have a place to go and he had supplies she could use on her hunt for Rahab.

"I'm fine!" she called out. She walked to the door, unlocked it and quickly stepped back.

John opened the door slowly and gently poked his head in. The light from his lantern cast a yellowish glow across the storeroom.

"I heard screaming. I was worried," John said, looking around the space.

Lexi had taken a seat back on the floor again, her pistol tucked in her lap. "It's all right."

"I'll let you get back to sleep, then," John said with a smile.

As the door was closing, Lexi called out, "Hold on!"

John craned his head back in. "Yeah."

"Ah, what time is it?"

"Oh, um, it's around five in the morning."

"Okay, thanks."

"You hungry? I can whip up something?"

"Actually, I'm thirsty."

"There's some water over in the corner, help yourself," John answered. He now half stood in the room. He pointed to a stack of bottled water.

"I was thinking of something a bit harder," Lexi said, a smile now stretching across her face.

A big drinker himself, John thought for a moment then opened the door fully. "It's noon somewhere, right?"

Lexi took the shot glass in her hand. The sides of it were slick from the over pour. One thing that hadn't changed since the lights went out was her love of partying and drinking alcohol. Before, hard alcohol wasn't her forte, but without ice and mixers, her favorites were no longer available. Determined to get the effect alcohol generously gave, she took to drinking whatever she could get her hands on. She looked at the bottle of Grey Goose and chuckled to herself. Before arriving in Crescent, she'd come upon a family. They had been welcoming even to the point of sharing their home-distilled spirits. The taste was repulsive, but she drank it anyway. She had never drunk paint remover before but only imagined that was what it tasted like.

She held it up and said, "What are we toasting to now?"

"Gosh, I don't know, what haven't we toasted to yet?" John asked, referring to the half-dozen shots they had already taken.

"I got one!" she said as she held her glass higher. "Death to all scumbags! May they die a slow and painful death!"

John raised his eyebrows in astonishment. He wasn't prudish, but Lexi's crude mouth and seemingly ruthless belief system did shock him.

She put the glass to her lips and with one gulp drank the vodka. "Ahh, that was good!" she said with excitement as she slammed the glass onto the bar.

John hesitated but soon followed and swallowed his shot of vodka.

"Hit me up, bartender," Lexi stated, sliding her glass towards John.

Ignoring her, he finally asked her an intimate and personal question, "Lexi, what happened to you?"

She leered at him and didn't answer.

"Why are you...so angry?"

"Is that a serious question? Really? Look the fuck around. Who wouldn't be angry?"

"I'm not."

"Then you're an idiot!" she snapped at him.

"Ha, I think you're cut off," John said, taking her glass.

"Wait, wait, wait, I'm sorry. That came off too..."

"Too angry," John quipped.

John walked away with the glass and placed it along with the bottle of vodka at the back of the bar.

"You're right, I'm sorry. You're not an idiot, I am. I just don't want to talk about…this," she said, motioning with her arms referencing the surroundings.

"You're going to sit at my bar, sleep under my roof, eat my food, drink my booze and not tell me who you are? You've been here a week and all I know is you drink a lot, work out and play with your knives."

Lexi thought about what John said for a moment and came to the conclusion he had a point. "You're right and I'm a bitch. I, um, I just don't like to talk about stuff, because doing so makes it seem real. Just sitting here like we've been doing for the past two or so hours talking about nothing but old movies, food, cocktails etcetera allows me to escape the fucked-up world we live in. It allows me to…forget."

John walked back and stood directly across from her.

"I've seen a lot of bad shit out there. I've seen what people are capable of. It's disgusting and revolting and I fucking hate it," she said.

"I can't say I've seen what you've seen out there because I decided to stay right here. Never saw the need to venture out beyond the town limits."

"Don't. Stay right here. It's a hot mess out there."

John grabbed the bottle and her glass and placed it in front of her.

She reached for it, but he slid it back just a few inches, indicating he wasn't quite ready to give it up.

The faint sound of John's rooster could be heard outside.

Lexi craned her head and looked at the nearest window; there she saw the morning's first light beaming through the thin metal blinds.

She turned back to John and said, "What do you want from me?"

"Nothing really, but if you're going to stay here, I'd like to know who you are, at least. I don't need to know the gory details. I'm just an old man who likes to know who I'm talking to. I look at it this way, before I lived my life not concerned about other people. I was one of those people who never listened to anyone. In a conversation, I took the time the other used to talk to think about what I was going to say. I never truly listened," John said, and then paused to think. "You know, that's probably why my marriage failed. I never listened; all I did was talk and talk."

"Like now?" Lexi joked.

John smiled and said, "Yes, like now. I'll just finish with this. After everything happened, I decided to listen. I finally told myself that life is fragile and all this can end at anytime, so why not take the time to get to know people. Everyone has a story."

Lexi sat staring at John as a feeling of sadness came over her. Not one to show her emotions anymore, she decided to respond in a gentler way than her typical crass self. "Fine, sounds like a fair deal. You're feeding and sheltering me, the least I could do is tell you who I am. The thing is, it's not exciting. In fact, it's downright boring, and the other shit that happened after was just plain horrid. But if telling you my boring story gets me another drink or two, I can do that," she said. A smile broke her stoic face.

John too smiled and looked at the young woman who sat in front of him. If he had to guess, he'd say she was in her late twenties. Her choppy and unevenly cut hair looked like it had been blonde once, but her dark brown roots had grown out so long that what remained of the blonde was now just on the tips. Her body was not skinny but slender with lean muscle. Her eyes were a light brown and her skin was a golden tan from the sun. Across her face, hands and arms he could see signs of cuts and bruising; she had definitely been fighting her way from wherever she came.

He slid the glass back to her, pulled the cork on the Grey Goose and poured her another shot.

She grabbed the glass quickly and was about to slam it down when he interrupted her.

"Hold on, sweetheart. What are we toasting to this time?"

Lexi again smiled and her answer came quickly. "Let's drink to getting to know one another."

"I like that."

They tapped glasses and drank.

Like before, she slammed the shot glass down and wiped her face. She could feel the effects from the vodka. "You have anything to snack on?"

"I can make some breakfast."

"I'm not a high-maintenance person, just a bag of chips or something will do."

"I wish, I ran out of...wait a minute, hold on," John said and quickly went into the back.

Lexi took the time of his absence to look around the bar. Her previous self would never have gone into a place like this, it would have been too 'redneck' or 'white trash' for her. Her past life was filled with nightclubs or trendy hip places. She never was one for dive bars or family-type bar and grilles, like the Mohawk. She spun on the stool till it faced a jukebox; without walking to see the playlist, she had a good guess the type of music that it held.

John returned almost giddy with excitement. "I almost forgot I had these," he said, holding up a large family-sized bag of Cool Ranch Doritos.

"No wayyyy!" She squealed like a kid.

"Yes, way."

"They're, like, my favorite."

"Mine too." He laughed.

"You, my friend, are definitely not a fucking idiot, you're the man!" she said loudly, barely able to restrain her excitement.

"And if you don't like that flavor, I also have…" He pulled a bag of regular nacho from behind his back.

"I'm not even high and I think I can eat a whole bag myself," Lexi excitedly said.

"Help yourself," John said as he opened both bags and placed them on the bar.

Lexi dove right into the chips. The texture and crispiness of the chips was still there. She only imagined they were past due, but she couldn't tell if the quality was inferior. Maybe it was because she hadn't had one in so long or she had forgotten how they tasted before.

"If you pull a Twinkie or HoHo out of your ass, I think I might have sex with you," Lexi joked.

"As a matter of fact…"

"No shit?" she muttered, pieces of chips falling out of her open mouth.

John turned to leave, stopped, turned back around and said, "Joking."

"I was joking too. I wouldn't have sex with you,

sorry. You're just a bit too old for me," Lexi said, stuffing a handful of chips into her mouth.

"Ha, sorry, sweetie, I look at you as the daughter type."

"Since you want to talk about who we are, you go first," Lexi urged.

"Nope, you go; I'm providing the feast and refreshments."

Filling her mouth with a few more chips, she began.

"I was born and raised in a not-so-shitty little town called La Jolla to a bitch of a mother who cared more about her next dinner party or socialite function than taking care of me or my sister. I have to laugh now; we were more like props for her. We were raised by a series of nannies over the years."

John just watched Lexi talk and all he could think was how someone could not love their children. He didn't have the experience, but he felt deep down that if he and his ex had had children, he would have loved them so deeply and given them everything.

"My mom was such a bitch she drove my dad away when I was six; my sister was a baby. He couldn't take her shit anymore."

"I'm sorry."

"I am too, I loved my dad. He won custody of us, but was killed in a small plane crash not two weeks later." She hesitated as she dreamt about the life she could have had. "Who dies in plane crashes? I mean, the odds are so slim that it was like fate said I was fucked from birth. God wasn't about to let me and Carey have a normal life."

"I don't think God—"

Lexi interrupted him, "No preaching, okay. I don't care if you believe in God, but any God that would allow children to be mistreated and this shit to happen can't be the nicest guy."

John cracked a grin and said, "Fair enough."

"Pour me another shot."

John obliged and listened through two more shots as she described her school days. He just looked at her and thought that deep down was a little girl who had been hurt tremendously throughout life. She had grown up relatively wealthy, but a child didn't really care about those things. A child values time and attention above all else. There she lived a life of poverty, one void of the love and nurturing a child needs from a parent. From what he gathered, she and her sister, Carey, had a very close relationship. Not wanting to leave her sister, she went to college locally. Then as if following a script of disappointment, her sister graduated high school and moved away to go to college. This deeply disappointed Lexi, but like a parent, she accepted it and decided that Carey was now old enough to take care of herself.

After her sister left, Lexi's life fell into a shallow and rhythmic repetition of work and partying with *friends*. With no goals or aspirations, all she had to look forward to was the next party. The relationship with her mother was estranged, they'd see each other for holidays, but Lexi couldn't wait to get to the bar and forget her life. Intimate relationships were nonexistent for her, with men coming in and out of her life quickly. When a man would show any sincere interest in her, she'd get rid of him. It wasn't that she didn't trust them, she didn't trust fate. Putting faith in love meant that she'd have to be vulnerable, and like other things in life, what happiness she'd experience would be wiped out by the pain of when that person would leave or disappoint her. Lacking any real connection other than Carey, she'd count the days until Carey would come into town.

John just listened. After first making a brief comment and seeing Lexi's irritated response, he just sat and didn't say another word. He filled her glass every now and then, but after a couple more, she slowed her drinking as she lost herself in telling her own story.

Her long diatribe stopped when she mentioned her sister's last visit. Shortly after that, the lights went out and the world changed forever. She sat, looked at her glass and drank it down swiftly.

John went to pour another, but she said, "I'll be right back." She abruptly stood, steadied herself from the alcohol-induced vertigo and marched towards the bathroom.

Lexi couldn't get to the bathroom quick enough; it was if she was having an anxiety attack. She hadn't told anyone so much. Opening up and being honest about who she was and where she came from was not a strong suit for her. She never had friends who took that type of interest. In fact, she liked them for that very reason. She had discovered it was easier to keep people at a distance because if she got to truly know someone, she would find herself not liking them.

When she walked back into the bar, John wasn't there. She looked around but couldn't find him. A loud clanging from the kitchen drew her attention; there she found him cracking eggs into a large skillet.

"Hey, you took a while in there."

She leaned up against the wall and joked, "Must have been those Doritos."

"You like fried eggs? I thought you could use some protein," he said as he looked over the eggs cooking.

"Love eggs, thanks. So, what's your story?"

"Not much to tell. Born just a few miles away, went to the local high school, married my high school sweetheart, got a job working for a lumber company but always wanted a place like this. My wife had other plans for her life; living in a small town became too much for her. She left me years ago, and instead of remarrying, I got this place. This here and all the loyal patrons have been my family since then."

"No kids?"

"Nope, never was lucky enough."

"Count your blessings. Believe me, we're pains in the asses."

"Oh, I don't believe that," he said as he gently slid a couple eggs on a plate.

She took the plate from him and smiled when she saw they were perfectly cooked sunny-side up.

He walked back and was cracking a couple more eggs for himself when she said, "Thanks, John."

"You're welcome, sweetie."

Lexi watched him work diligently. His large wrinkled hands firmly holding the spatula and the stained white apron tied around his waist made him look like a professional short-order cook, which in many ways he was, being the owner of a bar and grill.

"Anyone work for you?"

"Yeah, but I haven't seen them for weeks now. I heard they went to Portland."

With so much horror and cruelty in the world, here was a man who was gentle, sweet and generous. It was refreshing to meet someone like him.

Her journey since the EMP attack had destroyed

the power grid and brought society to its knees had shown her extreme examples of good and bad. It was as if when the rule of law and the blanket of legal consequences were ripped away, those who were deeply flawed or evil people exposed themselves. They were always there, but without the threat of arrest, they took to the streets. This also played out on the opposite side as well, with many good people willing to risk and sacrifice. Even though she had experienced both, Lexi kept her guard up.

She looked down at the eggs again. The special attention and consideration to not just make eggs for her but to make them sunny-side up said a lot about John. She liked him.

"You better go eat those before they get cold. Utensils are just to the left of the cash register."

Lexi left the kitchen, grabbed a fork and sat down. She went to poke the yolks but again looked at them. Never could she remember her mother doing this for her, but early memories of her father popped into her head. Her father was a busy man and was typically gone by the time she woke during the week, but her weekends were always special occasions. Not a Saturday would go by where she didn't have something special cooked for her; pancakes, French toast or sunny-side up eggs was the typical fare on the menu. When her father moved out, she still got to experience this but less, as he only had her and

Carey every other weekend. She resented her mother for driving her father away then denying him full access. It wasn't that she cared, it was done more out of spite and so she could get more money. However, her father was clever and, of course, had a great attorney. He eventually won full custody, but then life showed up and he was lost forever. When the thought of her father dying came to mind, she dashed it while simultaneously slashing the yolks with the fork.

John came out from the kitchen and said, "Good?"

"Yeah, they're great, thanks," she said, grabbing the bottle and pouring another shot.

"You're quite the drinker. How old are you?"

"Just turned twenty-nine, but I feel like I've lived three lives."

"Tell me about it," John said, tossing the apron on the bar and walking around to the front of the bar and taking a seat on a stool next to her.

She liked him, but when he sat not two feet from her, she reacted by scooting down a few inches.

John noticed and said, "Sorry."

Brushing off his apology, she asked, "So that's it for you, this place?"

"Ha, well, don't put it like that! That sounds so negative."

"Sorry, that didn't come off the way I was

intending."

"So you meet anyone as great as me on your journey?" he jokingly asked.

"No one as *great* as you, John! You're one of a kind."

"I wouldn't think so," he said, winking at her.

"You're a good guy and I have met other good people too, but they come and go."

"People just passing or you just passing through?"

"Both, but some just die. I'm fucking cursed, I think. I've been lucky. Had some good people help me and Carey, but shit just happens out there. You know, I can't believe shit hasn't gone down here."

"We've had some troubles but probably nothing to compare to what you've seen."

Lexi only nodded and continued to eat her eggs.

"Can I ask you something?"

"Oh shit, here it comes."

"Where's your sister? You talked so highly of her and mentioned she was with you before the attack."

Lexi turned and looked at him hard. "Some motherfucker murdered her. He thrust a knife deep into her chest."

John choked down his food and felt awkward about asking. "I, ah…"

"You asked and that's what happened. So you want to know why I'm here, sitting at your bar, eating your eggs and drinking your booze? This is a pit stop on my way to go kill that piece of shit."

"Is he nearby?"

"He's somewhere in Oregon, I know that."

"What's his name?"

"I doubt you know him, but his name is Rahab. He's the leader of a cult that Carey and I ran into in the California desert."

John thought for a moment to see if that name rang a bell, but it didn't.

"What happened?" John asked, knowing the question would elicit a charged response, but now he was curious as to what happened to this young woman.

"My sister had always been, I hate to say it, but the dumb one in the family. She always looked at life through rose-tinted glasses and went around without a damn care. It's so strange to think that we both came from the same DNA. She was always hurting herself. You know that person, the one that shit always happens to, not bad, but she was the one who always spilled her drink or made a mess. That was her."

John went back to listening as he slowly ate his eggs.

"She was always the one bringing lost dogs home, shit like that. But something changed in her after we were taken by Rahab and his people. She, for once, didn't just let things happen to her without thought. She decided then to take a stand, but that wasn't the time," Lexi said, pausing. She looked off in thought. "Her timing was always the worst." This comment was more of a thought expressed out loud. Her mind now swam with thoughts of her little sister. "Do you know that type of person, the one that shit always happens to?"

John nodded.

"She managed to get two weeks off for Thanksgiving. Of course, her luggage gets lost the moment she arrives and other assorted BS happens when she's in town. I have to laugh now, but I wasn't laughing then," she said, looking down, her mind going over the situations that frustrated her then. She longed for those moments, no matter how difficult or annoying they were. "You know, I'd do anything to have my sister and all her klutziness. I miss her, a lot."

John poured her another shot and slid it over.

Lexi grabbed it but stopped short of tossing it back. "For all her faults, my sister had a good heart and occasionally gave good advice." Lexi drank the shot and pushed the glass away from her.

"I know it doesn't mean much, but I'm sorry for your loss."

Lexi cocked her head and said, "I am too, but I have purpose now."

"Oh yeah, what's that?"

"Finding Rahab and his people and stopping them."

"Any other family?" John asked, shifting the conversation to something he hoped was less emotional.

Lexi paused and grunted. "Nope, some cousins sprinkled here and there, but I was never close with them."

"Friends?"

"Nope...well, I wouldn't call them friends, but they helped me escape from Rahab. They even invited me to go to Idaho; apparently they have a safe haven up there."

"Why not go?"

"Maybe, they were really nice people. Who knows, one day, we'll see," Lexi said, putting her head in her hands and slowly running her fingers through her hair. "Timing really is everything in life."

"I guess so."

"No, it is. Timing put me on the road outside of town so those Marines could help me. It also put me on the road headed to Vegas when we encountered Rahab's people. It's everything in life. Just take a minute away here or there and it changes the outcome."

John nodded as he thought about it.

"Carey was supposed to fly back on the fourth,

but she stayed because of me. She still might be alive if it wasn't for me."

"Or not," John said.

"Or might still be," Lexi countered sternly, not wanting John to deviate from the *story* she had told herself.

"You can't blame yourself."

"Of course I can and I always will. I was such an idiot then," Lexi said, slurring.

"Why did she stay?" John asked.

"She stayed to celebrate or at least that's what I called it," Lexi said. She gave John a look and grinned. "I know it might be hard to believe, but I used to be a big partier."

John raised his eyebrows and chuckled. "You don't say."

"I have a reason to drink now, it helps me forget, but back then I drank to just have fun."

He knew that wasn't true one bit.

"Are you sure you want me to continue my sad story?"

"It can't be all sad."

"Trust me, it is. This isn't directed at you per se, but why do men think they can take advantage of women?"

"What do you mean?"

"Just that men think women are objects to be fondled, fucked and discarded. It sickens me, and you know what, it was a man, a sick, depraved and perverted fuck that started this roller coaster for me. In fact, this man set me and Carey on the path that led to me sitting right here."

"Rahab was his name, right?"

"No, no, this was before Rahab. The piece of shit I'm referring to was my old boss."

John poured her another drink and pushed it towards her.

Lexi only looked at the glistening shot glass. The clear liquid looked inviting, but she withheld the temptation to drink. "You look at me and think you might know me, but I was a different woman not long ago. I was the typical Southern California blonde party girl with no real ambition or goals unless it led me to a rave, bar or house party. Looking back now, I wish I had prepared more. My life before was pointless and a massive waste of time. Anytime I encountered someone talking about being prepared, I gave them the standard eye roll. How could I have ever thought this whole fucking world would fall apart? Who knows this shit?"

"A few did."

Lexi shook her head and lamented, "I really wish I was more prepared; maybe I could have saved Carey. And I made so many stupid mistakes and then there's the bad luck," she said, holding her head low. She pressed her eyes closed and exhaled heavily.

John felt sorry for her. He hadn't lost anyone and his knowledge of the outside world was limited.

She lifted her head, grabbed the shot and poured it down her throat. Holding the glass in her left hand, she pointed it at John and said, "I can tell you this, I will never ever allow anyone, man or woman, to take advantage of me or any other innocent again."

"That's honorable."

She shot John a look and snapped, "Honor has nothing to do with it."

"So this former boss, what happened? What did he do?"

Lexi slid the glass back and said, "Fill it up and I'll tell you."

NEMESIS: INCEPTION is available on Amazon.

## ABOUT THE AUTHORS

**G. Michael Hopf** is the best-selling author of ten post-apocalyptic novels. He is a veteran of the Marine Corps, former Executive Protection agent and whiskey aficionado. He lives with his family in San Diego, CA
Please feel free to contact him at geoff@gmichaelhopf.com with any questions or comments.
www.gmichaelhopf.com
www.facebook.com/gmichaelhopf

**Angery American** has been involved in prepping and survival topics since the early 1990's. An avid outdoorsman, he has a spent considerable time learning edible and medicinal plants and their uses as well as primitive survival skills. He currently resides in North Carolina on the edge of the Pisgah National Forest with his wife of nearly twenty three years and his three daughters. He is the author of Going Home and Surviving Home.
Please feel free to contact him at chris@angeryamerican.com with any questions or comments.

Made in the USA
Middletown, DE
07 May 2017